"We have a deal, Emma," he said very quietly. "Don't we?"

She studied the hard planes of his face, marveling at how different he'd looked in those few moments he dropped his guard. He could be lying, a brilliant sociopath manipulating her, working up her empathy, sucking her in with charismatic charm. Or it could be the truth.

Either way, she was trapped. The only way out was to see this mission through, knowing that any misstep might cost her life.

"Yes," she said softly, placing her hand in his, "we have a deal."

Dear Reader,

We are all driven by our passions, our desire for things. But sometimes those needs become too consuming. They slide over a tipping point and grow dangerous, even life-threatening, and we begin to fear the power of what attracts us most.

Where is that tipping point in each of us? And do we need to cross that line before we can know if we are in control of our own desires? Before we can know if we are truly free? This is the problem my heroine, psychologist Dr. Emily Carlin, must face when she is contracted to profile the notoriously dangerous mercenary Jean-Charles Laroque.

Laroque is the embodiment of both Emily's desires and her deepest fears. And the closer she gets to him, the more power she gives him to destroy her. Emily will need to cross that line if she is to save both herself and Laroque… and find the freedom to love.

Loreth Anne White

Loreth Anne White

SEDUCING
THE MERCENARY

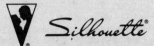

Silhouette®
Romantic
SUSPENSE

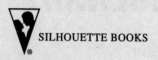 **SILHOUETTE BOOKS**

ISBN-13: 978-0-373-27560-1
ISBN-10:   0-373-27560-9

SEDUCING THE MERCENARY

Books by Loreth Anne White

Silhouette Romantic Suspense

Melting the Ice #1254
Safe Passage #1326
The Sheik Who Loved Me #1368
The Heart of a Mercenary #1438
A Sultan's Ransom #1442
Rules of Re-engagement #1446
Seducing the Mercenary #1490

*Shadow Soldiers

LORETH ANNE WHITE

was born and raised in southern Africa, but now lives in a ski resort in the moody British Columbian Coast Mountain range. It is a place of vast, wild and often dangerous mountains, larger-than-life characters, epic adventure and romance—the perfect place to escape reality. It's no wonder it was here she was inspired to abandon a sixteen-year career as a journalist to escape into a world of romantic fiction filled with dangerous men and adventurous women.

When she's not writing, you will find her long-distance running, biking or skiing on the trails, and generally trying to avoid the bears—albeit not very successfully. She calls this work, because it's when the best ideas come. For a peek into her world visit her Web site at www.lorethannewhite.com.

"Nearly all men can stand adversity, but if you want to test a man's character, give him power."
— Abraham Lincoln, 16th American president (1809–65)

Prologue

15:00 Zulu. Friday, November 8.
Ubasi Palace. West Coast of Africa

"The American embassy is being evacuated—all U.S. citizens are being advised to leave the country at once." The general paused. Silence permeated the room and hung heavy in the equatorial heat.

Jean-Charles Laroque nodded at his aide and walked slowly over the vast stone floor of his war room, toward the long arched windows cut into the walls of the palace he'd called home since he'd taken Ubasi by force just over a year ago. His leather boots squeaked softly, and his black dog, Shaka, moved like a shadow at his heels.

He clasped his hands behind his back and surveyed the dense jungle canopy that undulated for miles beyond the walls of his fortress, toward distant mountains shrouded in afternoon haze.

Four Americans had been killed in Ubasi, allegedly geologists with a Nigerian oil concern.

The killings had occurred simultaneously in different parts of Ubasi. The bodies had been gutted and strung from trees, left in the steaming sun for predators, *exactly* the same way his father used to exhibit his kills as warning to his foes.

Laroque's mouth turned bone-dry.

This had clearly been a coordinated operation, and it had clearly been intended to frame *him*.

As hard as he'd tried to shed the stigma of being the son of infamous South African-born mercenary Peter Laroque, the notoriety of his late father proved impossible to shake. And it followed him now with this gruesome display of bodies.

He pursed his lips in concentration.

On the heels of these murders had come even more disturbing news. His rebel allies who controlled the northern reaches of the Ubasi jungles had crossed into neighboring Nigeria, where they had raided the barracks of a U.S. oil corporation security outfit and captured five employees. Laroque's rebels maintained *these* captives were the killers of the Americans. They also maintained that the four dead geologists were in fact CIA agents who had been poking around Laroque's oil concessions in the north.

Laroque had been given nothing to prove this, just the word of his rebel leader with whom he had now lost contact as the cadre had entered the dense jungle at the foothills of the Purple Mountains. When the rebels reached base camp in a few days, word would be sent to Laroque and he could go and interrogate the captives himself. But until then, he had nothing.

He cursed softly in his native African-French.

Ubasi had just been welcoming back tourists. The U.S. embassy had recently reopened with two officers offering basic emergency service. Foreign currency was trickling in again. Telecommunications were gradually being restored. Even the electrical supply was becoming slightly more reliable. The war-torn economy was actually picking up for the first time in fifty years.

Now those same tourists were being told to evacuate.

And if those dead Americans were indeed CIA operatives, and if Washington thought Laroque was personally responsible for their deaths, that he had killed them as some kind of warning to the superpower to stay out of "his" country, and away from "his" oil, then some major form of retaliation was certain.

Ubasi was set to blow.

Adrenaline hummed through Laroque's blood as he turned to face the general, his dark mahogany skin gleaming in the equatorial heat. He touched Shaka's fur as he spoke.

"Contact every single foreigner who obtained a visa from the immigration office within the past six months," he commanded his general. "Order them all out. Shut the borders. I want as few innocent lives lost as possible."

Innocent lives like his sister's. Like her small children.

Bitterness filled his throat. It was always the innocent who suffered in this business of war. His business.

"There is also that science team sponsored by Geographic International—"

The image of the woman he'd seen in the street earlier that day once again took haunting shape in Laroque's mind. She'd stood out like a siren among the crowds that had gathered to greet him. Something about her had unsettled Laroque deeply. It was the way her violet eyes had looked at him, right *into* him. Cool fingers of warning raked through him, indistinct like mist over a jungle swamp. He blew them off sharply.

Perhaps she was part of the science team, perhaps not. It didn't matter. Either way she and every other foreigner would be out of his country by nightfall.

Laroque checked his watch. "The team should have landed in Ubasi nine hours ago. Turn them round, tell them they no longer have my sanction for their study."

"If they refuse?"

"Anyone who has not left for the airport by curfew hour tonight is to be brought here to the castle. Tell them it's for their own safety—Ubasi could turn into a war zone at any moment."

Laroque watched the heavy doors swing shut behind his general, and he clenched his jaw.

Someone was trying to manipulate him into a violent confrontation with the United States. He needed to know who and why, and he needed to know ASAP. If anyone defied his orders to leave Ubasi, he wanted them in his palace and under his watch, because it might just give him a lead, some small clue as to what the hell was going down.

And God help anyone trying to undermine him. Laroque would sacrifice *nothing* for his dream of freedom now. Because he had nothing left to lose.

And that made him the most dangerous kind of man.

Chapter 1

Nine hours earlier. 06:02 Zulu. Friday, November 8. Ubasi airport. West Coast of Africa

Perspiration dampened Dr. Emily Carlin's blouse as she neared one of two customs checkpoints.

There was no electricity in the cramped Ubasi arrivals room this morning. Fans hung motionless from the ceiling, the only light in the terminal coming from doors flung open to white-hot sunlight. Even at this early hour everyone was already dulled into slow motion by the rising temperatures and humidity.

The line of passengers shuffled slowly forward and Emily moved with it, people jostling her on all sides. She'd been informed Ubasi possessed no

X-ray equipment and the additional lack of power made it even less likely they'd find the knife strapped to her ankle under her jeans.

It was small protection, but she didn't expect much trouble. Her mission was simply to get into the beleaguered war-torn country wedged between Nigeria and Cameroon and assess the sociological situation. Most importantly, she was to compile a psychological profile of notorious mercenary Jean-Charles Laroque, known on this continent as Le Diable, a fierce and deadly guerrilla war expert, master military strategist, and now, a dictator.

She had exactly one week to do her job. Laroque's life depended on her assessment.

Just over twelve months ago the Parisian-born Laroque had sailed into Ubasi on a Spanish boat with a scruffy black Alsatian at his side, a rough band of mercenaries under his command, and a cache of black market weapons in his hold. After putting up a weak fight, the beleaguered Ubasi army had surrendered to Laroque.

Xavier Souleyman—the despot who had overthrown Ubasi's King Douala eight years previously and ruled the country with a bloody hand ever since—had escaped Laroque's capture and fled the country with the aid of a small band of loyalists.

Laroque had wasted no time moving into the royal palace, installing himself as de facto leader, and after negotiating with the rebels who had seized control of the northern jungles of Ubasi during

Souleyman's reign, Laroque had assumed *personal* ownership of massive tracts of land where his geologists had proceeded to strike oil—enough to potentially rival production in *both* Nigeria and Equatorial Guinea combined.

That fact alone had catapulted the once-forgotten country and renegade warlord instantly onto the world stage.

In less than a year Laroque had managed to broker unheard-of treaties with disparate rebel factions over the border in Nigeria and Equatorial Guinea—radical militants who opposed their own corrupt governments' financial ties with Western corporate interests in the Gulf of Guinea.

This placed Laroque in an exceedingly powerful anti-status-quo position. He now had the power to spark a major civil war in the region that could cut off oil supply to the rest of the world for decades to come— oil that had recently become critical to U.S. foreign policy, given the current tensions in the Gulf of Arabia.

On top of this, four deep cover CIA agents in Ubasi had just been slaughtered, their bodies displayed using the same gruesome signature technique once employed by Laroque's mercenary father as he'd cut an increasingly bloody swath across the continent before meeting his own violent end two years ago.

Laroque seemed to be sending a message to the U.S.: *Get out. Stay out. Or else.*

And here Emily was going in.

She mopped her brow with a damp and tattered

tissue as the queue inched forward again and heat pressed down.

Emily was a Manhattan-based expert in tyrannical pathology with a military background of her own. The minds of dictators, organized crime bosses, renegade warlords and murderous despots were both her passion and her professional specialty. Alpha Dogs, she called them.

She'd been contracted by the Force du Sable, a private military company based off the West Coast of Angola, to profile this particular Alpha Dog. The FDS in turn had been retained by a CIA-Pentagon task force in a clandestine bid to control the Laroque "situation." His threat in the region was becoming too great for corporate and political comfort.

The U.S., however, could in no way be overtly involved in a bid to oust the new Ubasi tyrant. Nor could the CIA trust its own at the moment—the source of the intelligence leak that had resulted in the deaths of the four CIA agents represented a grave internal security breach, which was why the FDS had been brought in.

Emily's assessment of *Le Diable* would be used by the FDS to formulate strategy. She needed to identify where the tyrant's psychological weaknesses lay—and in her experience, they *always* lay somewhere—and she had to pinpoint what fired him. While much was known about Laroque's military exploits in Africa, virtually nothing was known about the man himself.

No one knew what made him tick.

Emily's job was to figure out what did.

She also needed to ascertain whether taking him captive would exacerbate an already volatile situation in the Gulf. To do this, she'd have to determine how his subjects viewed him—as evil despot, or charismatic leader. Tyrants wore both stripes, and the last thing the U.S. wanted was to make the man a martyr.

If taking Laroque prisoner was not an option in Emily's opinion, the result would be death by assassination before midnight on Thursday, November 14.

Meanwhile, a team of FDS operatives was infiltrating Ubasi from the north. They would gauge the power of the exiled Souleyman faction, and start negotiations to back Souleyman in another coup to overthrow Ubasi. The FDS team on the ground would also get Emily out of Ubasi if she ran into trouble.

Emily didn't like the idea of swapping one murderous tyrant for another, but the U.S. did. Souleyman was easy to control. Laroque wasn't.

The oil business made strange bedfellows, she thought as she removed her water bottle from her bag, but politics was not her concern. Her sole interest was the Alpha Dog.

But while Alpha Dogs like Laroque were her intellectual thrill, they were also highly unstable—and dangerous. And she hadn't been on a mission for a while.

A combination of anticipation and anxiety shimmered through her stomach as the queue inched closer to the customs checkpoint. She uncapped her water bottle and took a swig of the warm contents.

She could not afford to screw this one up.

She couldn't afford to screw *anything* up. She'd left enough of a personal mess in Manhattan as it was. She *needed* this job. And she needed to do it right—for both professional and personal reasons.

Her nerves tightened as she glanced at the line of passengers on her left, the one with the rest of the Geographic International science crew—her cover. It was moving much faster.

She'd been separated from them by a soldier who called himself the "document man" and roughly shunted to the line on the right. Emily wondered if she'd have been assigned to the faster queue if she'd given the "document man" cash. But she was saving her two hundred dollars in bribe money for the big important-looking guy manning the customs booth ahead. She had another two hundred dollars U.S. stashed in her Australian-style bush boots as backup.

Perhaps she should have brought more.

She was uncharacteristically hot and edgy this morning, and it was not a sensation she enjoyed. Emily liked to stay cool and in control—always. She tried to shrug off her uneasiness, putting it down to the pathetic mess she'd left in New York. She was tired, emotionally drained, still reeling from her recent relationship fiasco.

The angry heat of humiliation once again flushed her cheeks. She'd been lured over the boundary between professional and personal, made to look like a fool. It had been a damn stupid mistake, and it would never, ever happen again.

She irritably swiped the sweat off her lip with the base of her thumb. This FDS contract could not have come at a better time. She wanted to put as much physical distance between herself and her ex—if she could even call him that—as humanly possible.

She needed to focus on someone *else's* pathology, not her own.

Emily was almost at the customs booth now, and her pulse quickened. She shot a look at the other line, saw the last of the science team leaving the terminal, and cursed silently.

While FDS leader, Jacques Sauvage, had hastily cobbled together a deal with their sponsors that allowed her to tag on to the Geographic International team, the scientists themselves had no idea why Emily was actually here, and they were under no obligation to coddle her. In fact, they'd been instructed by their sponsor to ask no questions at all. She cursed herself again. She should have forked over the damn bribe.

The customs official motioned for her to approach.

"Passeport?" he commanded in heavy African bass.

She handed it over along with her currency declaration form.

He flipped open her passport, glanced at her photo, looked up and met her eyes.

Her mouth went dry.

He smiled, teeth bright against gleaming ebony

skin. "And what have you got for me today, Dr. Sanford?" he asked in deeply accented English, using her alias.

She slid a hundred dollar bill across the counter, watching his face. He stared at the money, his smile fading.

She pushed another note slowly across the counter. "It's all I have," she said in English.

"Vous êtes Américaine?"

Her heart beat faster. It was patently obvious from her passport what her nationality was, and now he was refusing to speak English. *"Oui, je suis Américaine."*

"Raison de visite?"

A ball of insecurity swelled suddenly in her throat. "I'm here with the Geographic International science team," she said firmly, in English, wishing to hell the crew hadn't left without her. She unfolded and handed him another piece of paper that had the Ubasi palace stamp on it. "See?" She pointed to the signature. "We have permission from the Laroque government."

The official didn't even pretend to look at the piece of paper. His eyes continued to hold hers. "Currency declaration form?"

"I gave it to you, with the passport."

"Non—"

"I did! Look, it's right there," Emily said, pointing.

The man shook his head, raised his hand high above his head and clicked his fingers sharply. Two armed guards left their station at the exit doors and started making their way toward his booth. Emily's heart pounded wildly against her rib cage. "What's going on?" she demanded.

"There is a problem with your currency declaration," the customs official said in French, before turning to the next person in line. *"Passeport, s'il vous plaît?"*

"No, there isn't. Wait! You haven't even looked at my form. You—"

The guards took her arms roughly. *"Venez avec nous."*

Emily jerked back. "Why? Why must I go with you? Where to?"

But the guards hauled her briskly away.

"What about my luggage?" she snapped, dangerously close to losing her temper. "I haven't collected my bags yet."

But they remained mute as they forced her through a crushing crowd of people, all of whom studiously averted their eyes. The reaction of the crowd wasn't lost on Emily. She saw it as a blatant sign of fear of government authority. These people were terrified of Laroque's goons, she thought as the guards forced her into an interrogation room. She whirled round as they shut the door and locked it.

Stay calm. Breathe.

But no matter how Emily tried, she couldn't. The room was airless. The temperature had to be more than 100 degrees, humidity making it worse. Her jeans clung to her legs, her hair stuck to her back, and rivulets of sweat trickled between her breasts. Emily shoved the damp strands of hair back off her face. She *refused* to let this man or his country get the better of her!

She refused to let *any* autocratic male make a fool of her.

The heat of humiliation burned into her cheeks again. Damn, she was displacing her anger and she knew it. She needed to focus on this tyrant, not her ex. That's why she was here. She was a profiler for God's sake. She could do this.

She clenched her jaw, forcing herself to take stock. She still had her knife, her traveler's checks, her satellite phone, camera and, most important—her computer.

Anything she typed or downloaded into her laptop would be relayed via satellite to a monitor on the FDS base on São Diogo Island. It was state-of-the-art military communications technology, and it was how she would file her daily briefs, along with her final report on Laroque.

Just as she was thinking she'd be okay, the door banged open against the wall. Emily jerked in fright, heart pounding right back up into her throat.

The customs official loomed into the room. "I will see your checks and francs." He held out his hand, palm up.

"I…beg your pardon?"

He didn't budge.

Emily reluctantly opened the pouch strapped to her waist and forked over the wad of traveler's checks and francs she'd had to declare on the form.

The man thumbed through the wad slowly, mouthing the amounts as he did. He looked up sharply. "There is a discrepancy. The amount here is not the same as you declared on the form."

"It is. I—"

"This is illegal. You are smuggling currency. You will pay a fine of fifty thousand francs."

"What! That's ridiculous. That's…almost ten thousand dollars. I don't have that kind of money on me!"

"But you can get it, yes? You will have your *passeport* confiscated until you return to the *aéroport* with the francs for me personally, *ça va?*"

Emily looked at him, stunned. Without her passport she was a prisoner in Ubasi. And illegal. She wouldn't be able to obtain the visa all tourists had to buy in Basaroutou within twenty-four hours of landing. This was pure corruption. She cursed viciously under her breath. These men had targeted her because she was American, female, separated from her crew, and because she possessed expensive equipment. She was, in their eyes, a perfect candidate for extortion. And who the hell could she complain to? Their dictator, Jean-Charles Laroque?

She cursed again as the customs official abruptly departed, leaving the door swinging open. A guard waited outside with her bags, which no doubt had been searched.

Emily grabbed them from him as the guard took her arm, marshaled her toward the exit doors, and dumped her and her belongings unceremoniously onto the dusty streets of Basaroutou.

A riot of colors and sounds slammed into her, and for a second she just stood blinking at the chaos. People jostled her on all sides, dressed in everything from swaths of brightly colored fabric to tattered western dress and stark white tunics. Women carrying baskets on their heads hawked the contents, and on crumbling sidewalks vendors peddled everything from exotic fruits and strangely shaped vegetables to mysterious oils in brown bottles and weird-looking shriveled animals.

Poverty was clearly evident, as was a mélange of cultures. But the faces Emily saw were not ones of milling discontent. Her first impression was an air of industry and purpose.

She hadn't expected this, but then virtually nothing was known about Ubasi under Laroque's rule.

She shaded her eyes, sun burning down hot on her dark hair. Most of the buildings were dun-colored and flanked by impossibly tall, dull-green palms that rustled in the hot wind. Cerise bougainvillea clambered up walls pockmarked by years of war and roads were dusty and cratered with disrepair.

Emily squinted into the light as she searched for something that vaguely resembled a roadworthy cab.

Thankfully she still had what was left of her bribe cash in her boots. Passport or not, she had a job to do. She'd contact the FDS from the hotel and see what she could do about getting her papers back.

But as soon as she tried to elbow her way through the people thronging the sidewalks, she sensed a shift in energy that made fine hairs at the base of her scalp stand on end. She stilled, suddenly acutely cognizant.

There was a strange tension in the air. The mass of humanity around her was growing tighter, quieter. A dark anticipation began to throb tangibly through the crowd.

Emily's pulse quickened.

Soldiers were beginning to clear the street and line the road, holding people back with automatic weapons.

The air literally began to crackle with a mounting expectancy. Then the crowds grew suddenly hushed, and now she could hear only the rattle of palm fronds in the wind. Something was coming.

Emily's heart beat faster.

She began to look for exit routes. She knew from experience situations like this had a way of rapidly flaring into extreme violence. But anything vaguely resembling a cab was a good hundred yards off, and the crowds were closing her in even as her brain raced to comprehend what was going on. She was trapped, being wedged and jostled down toward the curb that edged the main street. She gripped her bags tight against her body and peered down the road, trying to see what was happening.

A burst of automatic gunfire suddenly peppered the air, and she jerked back as a convoy of military Jeeps rounded the corner at the bottom of the road. Soldiers triumphantly brandished AK-47s high above their heads, firing with abandon, the sound ricocheting between buildings as the convoy roared up the street.

Emily ducked as the vehicles neared her vantage point, but to her surprise, instead of fleeing in terror, the crowds around her surged forward, singing, ululating, chanting in such a strangely harmonious and resonant chorus it chased shivers over her skin.

Emily slowly stood, awestruck by the elemental effect of the primal sounds on her body.

The first set of Jeeps raced past in a cloud of fine dust. Then the haunting hush returned, silent anticipation thrumming in the humid air. Emily's heart began to pound like a drum as she leaned forward, trying to see all the way down the road.

A large open-topped military vehicle flanked by smaller Jeeps rounded the corner and crept slowly up the street. The crowd was so deathly silent that the only sound above the growl of engines was of the government flags snapping on the hood. As the big Jeep drew closer, Emily saw what they'd been waiting for.

Their leader.

Adrenaline dumped into her blood. She was seeing Le Diable in the flesh for the first time.

Jean-Charles Laroque sat high in the back of the vehicle, regal, utterly confident. Everything about him telegraphed power.

The sleeves of his camouflage shirt had been rolled back to reveal gleaming biceps. His shoulder-length

black hair was drawn back into a ponytail of dreadlocks that accentuated the aggressive angle of his
exotic cheekbones. He wore pitch-black shades under
an army beret cocked at a rakish angle over his brow.

At his side sat his faithful Alsatian, Shaka. The
dog's fur glistened in the sunlight, its teeth starkly
white against a pink tongue as it panted in the heat.

A hot thrill slid sharp and fast through Emily's
stomach.

The Jeep drew close, coming right up alongside
her, and a strange primal awareness prickled over her
skin. Emily could not have looked away if she tried.

Laroque turned his head, slowly scanning the
crowd, then his gaze collided with hers. His body
tensed visibly. He raised his dark glasses slowly,
looked right at her, *into* her, isolating her from the
crowd, cutting her from the herd like prey. He was
close enough for Emily to see that his eyes were ice-
green against burnished mahogany skin, and just as
cold, devoid of any humor or glimmer of kindness.

She could barely breathe. Her own eyes watered
as she met his gaze, unable to blink. Not wanting to.
The crowds around her faded into a distant blur, the
silence becoming a deafening buzz as her world
narrowed to focus solely on him.

Laroque shifted around in his seat, watching her
as his convoy crawled up the road…then he was gone.

Emily stood rooted to the spot, dust settling
around her as the crowd erupted in a riot of sound.
She tried to catch her breath.

What in hell had just happened here?

This man clearly had the adulation of his people. She hadn't expected that. Nor had she expected the effect he would have on *her.*

She swallowed, suddenly gravely uneasy with what she was about to do, with the very real impact her profile would have on this country, these people and that powerful man.

Because Emily wielded a power of her own.

Her professional judgment could kill him.

In less than one week.

Chapter 2

"They're gone, Jacques. The entire science team had left by the time I arrived at the hotel about two hours ago." Emily spoke in low tones on her encrypted satellite phone from her hotel room, hot wind whipping through the ragged banana leaves outside her window. "Le Diable's militia has ordered all foreigners out of the country before curfew." She glanced at her watch. "Which is *now.*"

It was already getting dark out, night descending like clockwork so close to the equator. There was also a thunderstorm brewing. "He seems to have shut down the borders in retaliation to the U.S. State Department advisory issued earlier."

"The State Department is worried about hostility against U.S. citizens," said the FDS boss. "No one has any idea those murdered Americans were operatives. They were deep cover."

"You think he's preparing for some kind of military strike?"

"Could be. I'll keep you posted. Our men can extricate you within two hours from when you sound the alarm."

"Apparently there were also five hostages taken from Nigeria by his rebels early this morning. That's the word here at the hotel," Emily said softly.

"We're on to that," Jacques said. "Looks like three of those hostages are U.S. nationals, and two Nigerian. They were taken from the security barracks of an oil outfit. Apparently Le Diable's rebels are transporting them into the Purple Mountains and heading toward the Ubasi border. No ransom demands. Not yet."

"Unrelated incident?"

"I never assume anything on this continent, but it could be. It's a common enough occurrence. In the meantime, it's fortuitous your papers were confiscated—it gives you a legitimate excuse to stay in Ubasi and defy the evacuation orders. See how long you can play it, and keep us updated."

"Gotcha."

"And, Carlin…stay safe."

Emily signed off, and bolted the louvered shutters

against the hot storm wind, anxiety tangling with
emotional fatigue in her body. Perhaps she wasn't
ready for this after all.

01:27 Zulu. Saturday, November 9.
Hotel Basaroutou, Ubasi

The night was intensely humid and close. Tattered
leaves slapped at her shutters while Emily tossed and
turned in fitful sleep. She'd swapped her T-shirt for a
skimpy camisole, and still she was soaked with sweat.

Her dreams that night were of Le Diable—dark,
sultry images full of smoke and heat and pulsing drums,
his green eyes piercing the blackness, his hands
touching her in ways she shouldn't even begin to
imagine. Her body was hot with desire—and panic. She
was breathless. Running. Trying to escape. Someone
was yelling at her, screaming that she *must* flee, that she
was in danger. She awoke abruptly, confused, drenched.

She opened her eyes, trying to gather her senses,
and realized with shock that the screaming was *real.*
Emily jolted upright in bed, heart slamming against
her breastbone.

Someone was banging on her door!

Before she could even think of grabbing her
sarong and getting up, the door splintered open and
crashed back against the wall.

She shrank back against the headboard as soldiers
armed with Kalashnikovs burst into her room.

"What…what do you want?" she demanded.

They said nothing. One tore back her mosquito netting, motioned with the barrel of his weapon for her to get out of bed. Another scooped up her phone, computer and camera—*all* her communication equipment. Without it she was totally cut off.

"Allez!" The big soldier pointed his weapon to the door. "Go!"

Emily was suddenly horribly conscious of the fact she was wearing only provocative lace panties and a sheer camisole that stuck to her breasts with perspiration. She held up her hands. "Just…just one second, okay? Please? One second. *Comprends? S'il vous plaît?"* She reached cautiously for her sarong, watching their eyes as she spoke. She covered herself as she slid awkwardly down from the high bed. She tied the sarong tightly over her hips with shaking fingers as she mentally scrambled for where she'd left her sandals and knife.

"Allez!"

"Okay, okay. My…my shoes—"

They grabbed her arms and shoved her barefoot toward the door, through the hotel and out to a waiting battery of Jeeps. That's when she knew she was in trouble—serious trouble.

02:03 Zulu. Saturday, November 9.
Ubasi Palace

Laroque paced slowly round the massive eboya-wood table that sat squarely in the center of his cavernous war room. There was still no electricity—the room was lit by flickering torches that sent shadows to shiver and crouch in corners.

Thunder boomed in the distance, making his dog growl and edge nervously up against his leg. Laroque reached down and patted Shaka's head, studying the wood pieces he'd laid out on the table in the style of old generals to mark the positions of his allied rebel troops, and pockets of resistance fighters—pockets that were growing mysteriously.

He frowned. His spies had informed him that Souleyman had set up camp in the jungle beyond Ubasi's eastern border. He was once again amassing power, but where his weapons and financing were coming from was an enigma.

At first Laroque had suspected the CIA. He knew Washington—along with the rest of the world—would be eyeing the massive oil reserves he'd recently discovered. And because of his rebel alliance, they would be seeing him as a serious threat in the region.

But if it was the U.S., and *if* those dead men were in fact CIA agents—their murders made no sense. Something else was at play here.

Anger bubbled through Laroque's blood. Again he cursed himself for not killing Souleyman when he'd had the chance.

His father would have.

His father would have seen Laroque's mercy as a mistake. And it was.

Souleyman had overthrown Ubasi's King Desmond Douala in a violent coup eight years ago. The king and his family had fled to France, the former colonial power, and Souleyman had declared himself leader-for-life, running the country by a process of extortion, bribes, torture and corruption, instantly silencing any political opposition with his notorious death squad.

It was how he had silenced Laroque's sister, and her children.

Laroque clenched his jaw. The mere *notion* that someone might be helping that bastard back into power filled Laroque's mouth with bitter repulsion.

He swore violently, strode to the huge arched windows, and glared out over the black jungle. Thunder rumbled again, and a gust of hot wind lifted the drapes.

It was for the love of the women in his life, the women he'd lost, that Laroque was doing this. He owed it to them. To his sister. This was her dream. And now that he'd started down this road, there could be no turning back.

But as he stared into the stormy blackness, it was the image of another woman that crept into his mind—the one he'd seen in Basaroutou. A strange hot frisson ran through him.

His general had told him that a U.S. national who had entered Ubasi with the science team had defied his orders to leave the country by curfew. Laroque had an odd feeling that the woman he'd seen in the street might be that person.

The hot wind gusted again, and anticipation rustled

through him as he caught the scent of the coming rainstorm. He checked his watch. It was just after 2:00 a.m. He'd find out soon enough who she was.

They were bringing her to him this very moment.

02:17 Zulu. Saturday, November 9. Ubasi Palace

The soldiers threw open a set of heavy studded doors and thrust Emily into a dimly lit, cavernous room. The doors thudded shut behind her, and she heard an iron bolt being dropped into place.

She blinked, trying to adjust her eyesight to the coppery torchlight. She could sense another presence in the room, but couldn't see anyone.

Then he stepped from the shadows, his famous black dog moving at his side.

Emily's heart stalled.

Laroque.

He said nothing, just raked his eyes over her from head to foot and back again, making her feel even more naked than she already was.

Her palms turned clammy, and her throat tightened.

He appeared even taller than the six foot three indicated in the FDS dossier she'd memorized. He was wearing the military fatigues she'd seen him in earlier, except now his hair hung loose to his shoulders. His ice-green eyes glinted in the light.

Emily choked down a rush of fear and awe as she forced herself into professional observational mode. She was being handed a rare opportunity here—face time with Le Diable, a tyrant in the making, right inside his lair. This man was her subject. She was here to study him.

But he was clearly appraising *her.*

She tried to tamp down the hot flare of déjà vu, the uncanny sense that she'd woken up in her own erotic nightmare.

Focus, Emily. You know the dominance psychology here. You can do this. You're still in control.

She cleared her throat. "I'd like to know why you brought me here like this?" she demanded in French. "And I'd like my clothes."

Laroque angled his head ever so slightly and the light played over his mouth. Was that a twitch of a smile—or anger—on his lips?

Emily straightened her spine, her movement instantly drawing his eyes to her breasts. She felt her cheeks grow warm.

He took a step toward her. "And *I* would like to know why you are in Ubasi." He spoke in perfect but beautifully accented English, his voice rolling out from somewhere low in his chest.

"I'm with the Geographic International—"

"No." He cut her short. "Why are you *still* here? Why did you not leave when ordered?"

She felt herself bristle. "I couldn't leave. Your customs official confiscated my documents and cash."

His eyes narrowed sharply, the chemistry in the room suddenly becoming darker, edgier.

"Why?" He said the word very quietly.

She swallowed. "He…maintained there was an irregularity with my currency declaration form."

"Was there?"

"Of course not. The man didn't even look at my form. It was extortion, pure and simple. He cut me from the crowd because I was female and had become separated from my group. He said if I want my documents back I must pay a fifty-thousand-franc fine. I don't have that kind of money on me. That is why I'm still here."

Muscles corded visibly along his neck, yet his voice remained measured, calm. "What was the official's name?"

Emily's stomach tightened. She didn't yet know where this man's trigger points lay, and she didn't like the way his cold eyes and level voice clashed with the invisible anger that seemed to be rolling off him in disquieting waves. This man was barely leashed violence. He was dangerous.

"His name," he insisted, even more quietly.

"I…I didn't get his name."

Laroque spun on his heels, reached for the communications device on his desk and punched a button. He issued orders in rapid Ubasian, his tone completely unemotional. Emily didn't understand a word, but there was something about his concealed tension that said it all—the customs guy was done for.

He released the button, turned to face her, the muscles in his neck still bunched tight. Silence descended on the room. It was then that Emily realized she was shaking.

"I'm sorry," he said, taking a step toward her, his voice suddenly as smooth and rounded as cream liquor over ice. "I do not condone extortion in any form, especially concerning a woman. I'll have your passport returned by dawn."

She lifted her shoulder in part shrug, part nervous reaction, his sexist comment not escaping her. "It's the way of this continent—"

"*Not* in Ubasi." He took another step toward her. "We will not manage to attain a democracy unless we root this sort of thing out now. I need my people to trust authority. Not fear it."

She felt her eyes widen.

He smiled, a quick and piratical slash against his dark skin, so fleeting she almost missed it. "You did not expect an apology?"

"Honestly? No…no, I didn't."

He pursed his lips, the light of flames shimmering in his eyes. It was an unexpectedly intimate look, a trick of the firelight. It reminded Emily of her state of undress, and the fact that he still had not offered to make her comfortable in any way. He still wanted something from her.

And he wanted her on edge to get it.

"What…what'll you do to the customs official?" she asked, wanting to probe his character, to use her limited time with him as best she could. But at the same time she was wary of pushing him.

"He'll be punished."

"How?"

He arched a brow. "You're interested?"

"Well…I…" *Tread carefully here, Emily.* "I've heard about the Laroque legacy on this continent, and I—"

"I am *not* my father. I will never be like him." Although spoken quietly his words were terse.

Emily noted his reaction. His father was a sensitive point. "I'm sorry," she said gently. "I didn't mean to offend you."

He regarded her intently. "You don't believe the customs official should be punished?"

Watch yourself, Emily. He's assessing you, just as you are him.

"It appears," she said, selecting her words with care, "that this man broke the law. Certainly justice should be done. But perhaps you could define the Ubasi version of 'punishment' before I can offer a considered opinion."

"Ah, a diplomat?" He smiled quickly, turned, strode away, then spun suddenly back to face her. "As well as a scientist."

He was closing in, yet giving her the illusion of physical space by walking away. This man was good. He understood people, psychology. And he knew how to use it. Most tyrants did.

"Your name is Emma Sanford—Dr. Emma Sanford. You're from New Jersey. You're both a sociologist and a psychologist."

Emily nodded. "That's correct." He'd gotten those details from the papers she'd had to file with the palace before joining the G.I. expedition. He was probably having her background checked this very minute.

She knew the identity Jacques had given her would hold. They always did, whether she went in as a nun, aid worker or reporter. Yet she felt as though Laroque could see right through her.

She folded her arms over her stomach as she spoke, and his eyes followed the movement of her hands. *Damn.* He was reading her defensive body language. The movement had come so instinctively in response to his question that she'd covered herself before she'd even realized it.

She didn't make mistakes like this. Laroque had managed to throw her way off center, just as he'd intended by bringing her here half-dressed in the dark of night.

And there was something in his penetrating gaze that made her intimately aware of her own femininity. He was all male. All in control. A very real and personal panic suddenly sliced into Emily. It caught her off guard and she fought to regulate her breathing.

She needed to stay focused. Professional.

"So what is a sociologist-psychologist doing with a team studying a volcano?"

She swallowed. She'd known this was coming next. Jacques's idea had been for her to play as close to her identity as was comfortable so that she could legitimately ask questions about Laroque's mental state without drawing suspicion.

"It's not just the volcano," she said. "We also wanted to look into the sociology of the villagers who live on the flanks of an active volcano. My specific role is to examine the psychology associated with dwelling on the shoulders of a geological monster that could erupt at any moment." She hesitated, watching for some kind of reaction in his eyes, but he gave away nothing. "I'm professionally intrigued by what rationalizations a society uses for remaining in that kind of danger. I also want to examine the mythology and religion that has evolved around living on a live volcano."

A genuine interest crept into his eyes. It was the first real sign of emotion in him, and it emboldened her a little. "That's basically my goal here in Ubasi— to do that research and to compile a series of articles for our sponsor's magazine." She allowed her eyes to flicker briefly to the side, feigning a touch of coyness. "I was also hoping to examine life in Ubasi under the new leader. I'm told things are improving in the country," she said, forcing a soft smile.

He said nothing.

She tilted her head, met his eyes and deepened her smile, fully aware of what she could do to a man, if she wanted. "You're an enigma," she ventured. "A French soldier of fortune who came out of the blue to take an African country for himself. It's a bold and fascinating story." She stepped closer to him. "That's more than an article, Your Excellency," she said, using his official title. "That's a book."

His eyes flared briefly. "I gave no sanction for a book."

"I know. A book is my *personal* interest, an adjunct to my work with the Geographic team. I'd been hoping to request an interview while I was here."

This is where feminine flattery should work on an autocratic personality. This is where the Alpha Dog should be seduced into talking about himself. But Emily had just succeeded in unsettling *herself*—because not only was she physically ruffled by this man's proximity, the idea of a book on the warlord-turned-tyrant was something she actually wanted beyond this FDS mission. She was hewing too close to her own desires.

He studied her quietly, shadow and light playing over his features. For a moment she thought she glimpsed a softening in his eyes, a shimmer of sadness, even, a small window opening to the real man inside.

"I see." A ghost of a smile tipped the corners of his lips. "For a moment there I thought you were going to compare living on an active volcano to life in Ubasi under my rule."

Emily wasn't sure whether she was expected to laugh, or if he was playing her, just as she was playing him.

Confusion coiled inside her. Thunder crashed, right above the castle this time, unleashing the full brunt of the storm. Rain lashed against the walls, and wind howled, billowing curtains and ferrying a mist of fine droplets into the room.

He held out his hand in a sudden gesture of magnanimity. "It's late. Allow me to offer you accommodation, Emma—may I call you Emma?"

"I…yes, of course."

"Stay in my palace, be my guest for the night while we sort out your passport issue."

Hope fluttered in her chest.

"You will then leave Ubasi before noon tomorrow."

Her heart sank right back down. "So…there's no chance of an interview, then?" she asked, trying to push her luck.

He held her eyes for several long beats, as if deciding whether to even answer.

"What good would a book do me, Emma?" he said.

She decided to play her wild card. It was dangerous, and she knew it, but she'd glimpsed the little chink in his walls, and being bold enough to go for those barely perceptible vulnerabilities was what had made Emily the uncanny success she was at psychological analyses—so successful, in fact, her peers often joked about her being psychic. Plus, she was running out of face time with Laroque. If she didn't move now, she'd lose her window completely. She'd fail her mission.

"A book could show people that you are not like your father, Your Excellency."

His mouth flattened and his eyes narrowed to slits. He took a step closer to her, and she felt herself tense.

"It's not the truth the world wants to read,

Emma," he said darkly. "What is true is less important than what is widely believed. People prefer to believe in monsters."

"Monsters like Le Diable?" She watched his eyes. "Or monsters like Peter Laroque?"

He came close to her, very close, and he lowered his voice to a soft murmur near her ear. "What if I *am* like him, Emma?"

Heat began to burn low in her belly. But she didn't shy away from the penetrating intensity in his eyes, or from his closeness. "That's your fear, isn't it?" Her voice came out a whisper. "You're afraid that deep down somewhere you *are* like him. But I don't believe it." And she didn't. She was going on a raw gut feel here, taking one hell of a gamble. "Let me stay, Your Excellency," she said gently. "Give me the interview time. Please."

A muscle pulsed under his eye.

He leaned down farther, his mouth coming very close to hers. "What do you *really* want from me, Emma Sanford?"

She shivered at the sensation of his breath, warm against her skin, and for a nanosecond she wasn't sure *what* she wanted. Her heart began to race so fast she could barely breathe. She tried to moisten her lips. "Just…the interview time."

He studied her in silence that vibrated like electricity between their bodies, his eyes probing hers, searching for something. Emily felt herself begin to burn from the inside out.

"I need to know something first, Emma," he said softly, his eyes lancing hers. "Do you understand just how dangerous things are in Ubasi right now?"

Oh, boy, did she ever. In more ways than one. She was in trouble. Every warning bell in her system was clanging for her to step away from him. Right now. Run. Flee! This was a man who could convince a woman to cross the line into sin with one little crook of his finger. This was exactly the kind of man she *must* avoid, the kind of man who got her into personal trouble.

Except this time she couldn't flee. This time the man she feared on a very personal level *was* her professional mission. And this time, her life might be on the line.

Whether he was like his father or not, Emily had little doubt Le Diable would kill her if he learned she had come to destroy *him*.

"I do," she whispered, eyes burning from the effort of sustaining his gaze without blinking. "I know exactly how dangerous."

Chapter 3

A dark whisper of warning breathed through Laroque as her violet eyes held his steadily. "I saw you," he said, watching her carefully. "In the street this morning."

A nebulous look swam through her eyes. "I know."

Something rich and dark slid through his stomach. She'd felt the same connection, he could read it in her eyes, hear it in her voice. Every last strand of primal DNA in his body fought to override rational thought at this moment.

He loved the way her hair fell in a dark tangle almost to her waist, the way freckles ever so faintly dusted the pale skin over her nose. And he was particularly attracted to the sharp intelligence that sparked in her unusual eyes. This woman presented challenge.

And *nothing* fired Laroque like a challenge.

It fueled a voracious appetite in him—for victory, dominance. It made him want to play the game.

There was no doubt in his mind that he'd take her physically, should she dare offer.

But he didn't trust her.

He'd be damned if he didn't *want* to, though. The notion of sharing his personal story with her was strangely compelling.

He'd never told anyone his life story before. He'd borne his scars solo since the age of thirteen, pretending the opinions of others never bothered him.

But they did.

Deep down, if he really was truthful, Laroque wanted people to understand that while he'd learned the art of guerrilla warfare and the techniques of torture and death from his father, while he'd been forced to follow, and depend on, and fight with Peter Laroque for his very survival, he was not at all like him.

Yes, he'd become a mercenary, because it was what he knew, and he'd become very good at it. But he had his boundaries. His game was always an ethical one. And what he wanted for Ubasi—for the entire region—was good. Bold, yes. Overambitious, perhaps. But it was for the benefit of the majority who lived in increasingly abysmal conditions in contrast to the rapidly growing oil wealth of a few corrupt leaders.

The romantic part of Laroque actually *wanted* to believe that this woman had been dropped into his life like an angel.

But he wasn't a fool, and he did not believe in co-incidences. He also had trouble believing her science crew would just abandon her like this.

He needed to check her out. Thoroughly.

In the meanwhile, he needed to be sure she was safe. His castle was the best place for her tonight.

"You'll agree to the interview, then?" Her voice was midnight velvet, soft and powerful at the same time. It was the kind of voice that made a man aware of his sex. And that made her potentially dangerous.

"You're welcome to stay the night," he said bluntly.

Surprise showed in her eyes. "Is that all?"

"That's all. I'll have my men show you to the guest quarters. They'll escort you to the airport before noon."

He stepped back and summoned his guards.

Langley, Virginia. CIA headquarters

CIA director Blake Weston pored over the reports on his desk. The death of his men in Ubasi ate at him like acid.

He rubbed his face, inhaling deeply.

He had what appeared to be an extremely serious intelligence breach on his hands. His agents in West Africa had been deep, deep cover. The exposure of their identities indicated an information leak, and it could only have come from the *inside*. At least this is how it would be viewed in Washington. He pinched the bridge of his nose.

Blake was new to this top job, and the White

House was watching carefully to see how he handled his first major crisis. His agency had to be seen to be acting swiftly, decisively and ruthlessly to root out any possible mole. Blake was also aware that his career depended not only on his actions at this critical juncture, but on the political *perception* of his actions.

Which is why the Laroque-Ubasi situation had been instantly outsourced to the FDS, an objective organization, while the CIA could be seen to be dealing with its own internal security issues. Blake had no doubt the FDS would effectively eliminate Jean-Charles Laroque and pave the way to stability in the Gulf of Guinea.

But that didn't solve the disclosure of his men's identities. *That* was the problem that burned him. That was what would come back to haunt him.

He shoved his chair back, stood, unscrewed his bottle of pills, popped two into his mouth. This clandestine cooperation with the Pentagon only confounded things. He'd been put hands-on in charge of the new joint task force, and any failure would reflect directly on him. He chewed his medication slowly, thinking. This business was full of mirrors and shadows and smoke—one never really knew who or what one was dealing with. Or what the agenda was. He could use this to his advantage.

But getting off this particular tiger was going to be tricky. Maybe impossible. It could even cost him his life. If Blake was to have any chance of actually riding this one out, Laroque *had* to take the fall for the agents' deaths.

If Laroque died with Washington believing the tyrant had somehow discovered the CIA agents' identities on his own, the mystery—all the niggling questions—would die with him. Then Blake's problem would simply disappear.

There was just one little hitch—the profiler. The FDS had insisted on this approach. Blake had been dead set against it. He didn't need some academic from New York declaring the tyrant fit for capture, he needed him *dead*.

He glanced at the calendar on his desk.

The FDS profiler had less than one week to make her move. It had damned well better be the right one.

03:17 Zulu. Saturday, November 9.
Ubasi Palace

Emily lay on the king-size bed staring at the impossibly high ceiling. The door had been bolted from the outside. When she'd protested, the guards had said it was for her own safety. The balcony was too high to climb down. She'd checked.

She was imprisoned like a damn princess in a castle tower.

Her bags had been delivered to the room, but her computer, phone, camera and knife were all still missing. Emily had little doubt Laroque was going through her things with a fine-tooth comb, checking out her story—her identity.

She told herself she shouldn't worry. It was state-of-the-art military issue, and everything was en-crypted. The FDS techs were among the best in the world. They'd have been careful not to leave digital clues. Laroque wouldn't find a thing.

So why didn't she feel more secure?

She figured the only reason she was still here in his castle boudoir was so that he could thoroughly check her cover story. Perhaps he hadn't believed a single word she'd said. She wondered if she'd even see him again.

Emily tossed irritably on the Egyptian cotton sheets as the wind moaned up in the parapets and rattled at the French doors on her little stone balcony.

The more she thought about it, the more she really liked the idea of a book. Laroque exhibited classic Alpha Dog pathology, yet he'd only recently become a dictator, which meant she had an opportunity to witness a monster-in-the-making. Scoring a one-on-one interview with Le Diable would not only secure her FDS mission, it could earn her academic prestige down the road.

It would give her something to take back to New York.

Emily desperately needed some sort of profes-sional—and personal—validation after being so thor-oughly humiliated by her ex and her peers. Anger surged through her at the memory. She sat up abruptly in the bed, forced out pent-up breath with a puff of her cheeks.

She did *not* want to go back to New York a failure.

The fiasco she'd left at home had forced her to question everything about herself, every choice she'd ever made in life—from her career to the men she dated. And she really didn't want to face those questions. Not now. Not yet. Maybe never, if she could help it.

She wanted excitement, adrenaline, something big to focus on right now, other than herself.

This wasn't running, she told herself. Sometimes you just needed distance.

She slid off the bed, snagged the water jug on the dresser and poured herself a glass. She took a swig but the liquid balled in her throat.

Her eyes began to burn and hurt tightened her chest.

She'd trusted her ex.

Hell, she'd even thought she loved him. But it had just been a game—a bet he'd taken with his colleagues that he could not only bed the brainy ice queen, but make her fall for him.

She plunked the glass down, shoved her hair back from her face and cursed viciously.

She *had* fallen for him. His name was Dr. Anthony Dresden. He was much older, an esteemed university professor who did consulting at *her* clinic. Not only had he made a mockery of her, but he'd lured her across a line she should never have dared cross—that line between personal and professional. A vital line in a field like hers.

What made it worse was the fact she'd once confided to Anthony that she was concerned about her consistent attraction to dominant and physically powerful males—men like her dad. She'd told Anthony she was beginning to think she subconsciously found ways to sabotage her relationships with men like this as soon as they showed signs of getting serious. That's why her relationships never lasted more than eighteen months. She invariably grew afraid that if she committed wholly to the alpha guy in her life she'd be trapped. That he'd undermine her independence and ultimately quash her. Like her dad had quashed her mother.

To death.

Emily was deeply afraid of not being in control, always. Because in her heart, Emily was terrified that she was really just like her mom. Weak.

Dr. Anthony Dresden, a man she'd once respected on so many levels, had used her secret fears against her.

He'd taken a substantial monetary bet one very drunken night over dinner with a group of his—*and her*—male colleagues. He'd wagered he could seduce the brainy ice queen—that's what they called her— and make her fall for him. He'd bet he could date her longer than any of her previous relationships. He'd told his friends that it was more than sex for Emily, you had to get her at her own game, a mind game.

It was pure betrayal.

When their relationship had gone over that eighteen-month hurdle, Emily's heart had begun to feel light, as if a huge weight had been lifted from her. She thought she might be truly in love, that Anthony was *the one*.

Tears slid hotly and angrily down Emily's face.

He hadn't collected on the bet.

When she'd found out about it via the grapevine, she'd been devastated. Anthony told her he'd called the bet off because he'd come to care deeply for her. He said it had been a lark, something he should never have allowed to happen. He'd pleaded with her for the relationship to continue. That's what made it worse—the fact that he said he really did love her.

All he'd done was reinforce her deep-rooted pathological fears. Because in a powerfully intellectual and physically subtle way, Anthony was an alpha himself. She'd fallen for his calculated seduction, and he'd used her own mind against her. And everyone who mattered in her career knew about it.

Emily threw herself back onto the pillow and closed her eyes tight. No, she could not go home.

Not yet.

Not until she'd proved something to herself.

05:45 Zulu. Saturday, November 9.
Ubasi Palace

A soft peach bled into the ink sky. Monkeys stirred in the branches below, and the sound of birds rose in a soft chatter. Laroque stood on his balcony, hands flat on the balustrade, surveying the dark jungle canopy.

The storm had blown through, and he was enjoying the rich scent of fecund earth. In a few hours the forest would be an oppressive place, steaming under the sun's fire. He liked these predawn hours best.

He hadn't slept, but he was used to not sleeping. He'd learned since a boy how to push, and keep pushing, to rest only when the battle had been won. He wouldn't be alive otherwise.

"Sir?"

He spun round to face Mathieu Ebongani, the technician who'd been busy with Emma's equipment.

"Mathieu, did you find anything?"

The tech stepped onto the balcony. "Her ID checks out."

"What about her equipment?"

"It's beyond my scope, I'm afraid. Her satellite phone and computer are fitted with highly sophisticated GPS and encryption technology," he said. "We're going to need Ndinga if you want to try to decode it."

"Is the technology consistent with a science mission of this nature?"

The tech's mouth twisted. "It looks more state-of-the-military to me." He paused. "It's her laptop that worries me. It appears to be communicating at a low-level-signal strength with another off-site station, even when turned off."

"GPS?"

"No, this is something different." He hesitated. "I haven't seen anything like this before. We'd learn more by opening the hard drive up in a forensic environment, but again, we'll need Ndinga and his team for that."

Laroque's pulse quickened. "What about her computer files?"

"Encrypted, but she does have a photo in there that I could access."

"Photo?"

"From the Parisian Press archives. The caption says it's you at age thirteen being taken from the hospital by your father."

A band of muscle tightened sharply across Laroque's chest.

His mind was yanked instantly back to a day he'd rather forget. His mother had been famous. She was always in the tabloids, and by default, so was he, the young boy hanging on to the skirts of the glamorous African model, or so it had looked to the world. It was logical Dr. Emma Sanford would have dug one or two of those out, especially if she wanted to work on a book. Yet it made him feel strange. Vulnerable. Especially *that* specific image.

Did she know it represented the turning point of his life?

"Anything in her e-mail?" he asked, his words unnecessarily clipped.

"Only correspondence with Geographic International headquarters."

"Thank you. Keep her equipment for Ndinga's return," Laroque said, dismissing his tech.

He turned to watch the peach sky deepen to burnt orange, then blood-red as the fiery ball of sun crashed over the Purple Mountains in a wild symphony of color. He breathed in deep. He loved the African sky. It was bold. Confrontational. Always changing.

It defined *him*.

He hadn't been born here, yet this place pulsed rich through his blood. His mother was an Ubasi native, his father a third-generation South African of Dutch heritage. Laroque himself had been born and schooled in Paris, but from the age of thirteen this continent had been his heart and soul.

People from other parts of the world didn't understand the differences, the laws of this vast and elemental land. They *couldn't*. The things that happened here just weren't in the lexicon of the West.

It made him mad…and, strangely, glad. He was as conflicted about this place as it was conflicted itself.

But he did know that if Ubasi and the rest of the Niger Delta was to survive, thrive even, he needed to bridge that vast gap between Western ideology and African. The rebel oil alliance was the starting point, the foundation of something big, a local OPEC and an army with some real negotiating power for the people of the Delta.

He wondered just what part in this unfolding melodrama Emma Sanford was to play, if any. There was a chance she was telling him the truth, but things weren't adding up well enough to make Laroque comfortable.

Her computer equipment had only raised more questions.

If she was broadcasting he wanted to know to whom—and why. He needed to hang on to her gear long enough for Mano Ndinga, his top IT genius, to return and look into it.

Laroque checked his watch.

Mano and his team were busy installing a network at the Nigerian base of one of Laroque's allied rebel militias. They'd be back in roughly four days. Laroque couldn't hold Dr. Emma Sanford prisoner until then. It would cause an international outcry.

He could just ship her out of the country. However, if she *was* some kind of informant, she might be a vital link to whatever was going on behind the scenes in Ubasi. He'd be a fool not to milk that angle—it was the only lead he had. And if worse came to worst, she might end up a valuable negotiating tool.

She'd have to stay on her own volition.

He'd have to make it *her* choice.

He drew the morning air deep into his lungs again, and breathed out slowly. If the lady was playing a game of deception, she was good. But he'd show her that he was better.

And keeping one's enemies close—very close—was never a bad idea.

8:07 Zulu. Saturday, November 9.
Ubasi Palace

A loud rapping on the door ripped Emily from sleep. She jolted upright, squinting as she tried to focus. Bright bars of sunlight streamed through shutters, throwing slatted patterns on the walls. Her head felt fuzzy, her mouth dry.

The banging continued, louder.

She stumbled out of bed and headed toward the door, belting the silk robe she'd found behind the bathroom door tightly around her waist as she went. She pulled on the brass handle, and it gave—the door had been unlocked from the outside. She drew it open cautiously, shoving her tangle of hair back from her face as she did.

Muscled pecs under a snug-fitting crisp T-shirt greeted her at eye level. She stared numbly, her brain trying to kick back into gear. She lifted her eyes slowly and met his clear, penetrating gaze. Her stomach somersaulted, and she grounded herself by reaching for the door handle, his eyes instantly tracking her movement. Did this guy not miss a damned thing?

"Good morning," Laroque said in his exotic African-French accent, a smile reaching right into his luminous green eyes, making them sparkle with unspeakable mischief.

The effect rocketed through Emily like dynamite. And damned if her cheeks didn't flush. She reached up to smooth down her hair.

"You slept well?"

"I…yes. Thank you." It sounded trite. She'd been abducted and locked in a turret, for goodness' sake. "I was tired. I *was* dragged here at 2:00 a.m.," she added defensively. "What…time is it, anyway?"

He held up her passport. "Time to leave Ubasi."

She stared at her passport in his hand, her ticket to freedom.

She reached up to take it from him, but as she tugged at the passport, he held tighter, his fingers connecting with hers, the sensation electric. Emily's breath caught and her eyes whipped to his face.

"I have a proposition," he said. "Take the passport, and leave Ubasi before noon. Or—" He paused, watching her way too intently for comfort. "*I* keep the passport, and you stay and interview me. Your choice. My terms."

Her heart was now racing so fast she could barely breathe. "Your…terms?" Her voice came out thick.

"Stay in my palace, under my constant guard. If we do venture beyond the fortress, you do not leave my side. Understand? Not for one instant. No exceptions. It's for your own protection, of course."

Emily appeared to be incapable of disconnecting from his touch, of letting go of her passport, her ticket to freedom. Her mind reeled. She should leave, for her own good. Perhaps she wasn't yet mentally ready to handle this man and the strange seductive power he had over her.

Then she recalled the mission, why she needed to succeed. She thought of New York, of her ex, of the utter humiliation and pain that awaited her.

She'd be Laroque's voluntary captive. She'd have exclusive access to Le Diable in his inner sanctum, an extremely rare opportunity to watch one of her Alpha Dog subjects at work. She'd have access to information that could help the FDS.

This was an opportunity that might never present itself again.

This was what she wanted—wasn't it?

A dark, sensual excitement tangled with rising adrenaline as conflict raged through Emily. He was making it *her* decision. He was making her a partner in her own captivity. It was a power play.

Laroque could destroy her if she stayed. He would kill her if he found out who she was working for.

This is life and death, Emily. This is the real thing. Wake up, here, think straight.

Logic screamed at her to leave, screamed that she was basing decisions on flawed reasoning, on personal issues, not professional ones. Logic told her that at some level she was dangerously attracted to this subject, and it reminded her of all the trouble she'd ever gotten herself into when she'd tangled emotionally with A-types. And those men in her past didn't even begin to hold a candle to the kind of power and sexual charisma Laroque possessed.

Neither were they killers.

But she *couldn't* leave.

"Keep the passport," she said quietly, dropping her hand to her side.

His smile was sharp and fleeting as he whipped the passport away and handed it to a sullen guard who materialized from the shadows at his side. Emily had a sinking sense that she'd just made a mistake. A grave one.

And now there was no turning back.

Chapter 4

Emily cinched the belt of her robe tighter around her waist, pulling herself together. She had less than six days left to file her report on Laroque, to decide whether he would live or die.

If she failed to submit by the deadline, Jacques's men would move in, and he'd die, anyway.

She moistened her lips. "My equipment is missing. I'll need it if I am to record our interview."

"We're looking into it," he said.

Yes, I'm sure you are, she thought.

"In the meantime, I'll make sure you have a replacement laptop."

"I need my phone. I *must* report in or my team will

be worried. They'll contact the U.S. State Department, alert the embassy in Cameroon, and—"

He held out a stubby satellite phone as if he'd been anticipating every word. Maybe he had. Maybe he didn't believe her at all. Perhaps he'd found something in her computer, but not enough to condemn her outright. Her eyes shot to his, and nerves once again skittered like butterflies around her heart.

"One call," he said.

"Why only one?"

"Things are unstable in Ubasi. I'm limiting communications."

"But why—"

"We agreed, Emma, my rules."

The nerves tightened in her chest.

"If you wish to change your mind—"

"No," she said, reaching for the phone, careful not to connect with his skin again. "I'm fine with that."

He waited.

"You…want me to call here, right now?"

"Is that a problem?"

"No, it's not," Emily said, racking her brain for the mobile number of Max Rutger, the science team leader. She punched it in slowly, praying it was correct. She put the phone to her ear. It rang once. Twice. Three times. Her mouth turned dry. She flicked a glance to Laroque.

He was watching her intently.

"Hello?"

Relief slammed through her at the familiar sound

of Max's voice. "Max! It's Emma." She couldn't give him a chance to speak, to blow her cover. "The Laroque government has come through on my passport issue. I—"

"Thank God," he interrupted. "We heard you had problems and felt terrible about the note we left when—"

Perspiration prickled under her scalp. "Max, I'm fine, really. Jean-Charles Laroque has apologized to me personally. And you know that project I was working on?" She didn't dare give him a chance to get a word in edgewise. "Well, he's granted me one-on-one interview time for the book. Isn't that great? I'll be staying at his palace as his guest, but communications are limited at the moment, so will you please let *the office* know that I'm still working on…my personal project while you guys wait things out in Cameroon? Let them know at once, please, Max. And tell them I'll be in touch as soon as I can. Thanks, Max." She quickly cut the call, heart pounding, palms damp, praying that Max would get the hint to call their sponsor who'd notify Jacques. She handed the phone back to Laroque.

His eyes were flat as he took it from her. "That was…brief."

She said nothing. She could hear the rush of her own blood in her ears.

"We'll discuss the parameters of the interview over breakfast," he said abruptly, his eyes flicking over her body. "As soon as you're dressed." He turned and started down the corridor. "My men will escort you down to the terrace," he called over his shoulder.

And he was gone, his black Alsatian moving like a ghost in his wake, leaving only the hollow tap of boots echoing down the castle corridor, and the click of his dog's claws on stone.

Emily slowly released the breath she'd been holding.

"I want to know when Mano will be back ASAP." Laroque delivered his words with staccato precision into the phone. "Tell him I have an important job waiting." He hung up, reached for his coffee cup and stretched his legs out under the garden table. He sipped from the white china as he watched a blue crane walk along the edge of the castle's rock swimming pool.

Shaka's ears twitched at the sight of the bird. Laroque reached down absently to stroke his pet, acknowledging his dog's restraint. His suspicions about Emma were even stronger now. But the telling evidence might come once his IT expert returned. Meanwhile, he wanted to find out as much about her as possible, as soon as possible, because he had a sense that the longer she stayed, the more damage she could do.

Emily paused at the entrance to the garden.

The man and his dog waited for her on the lowest terrace overlooking a vast swimming pool. Laroque's back was to her. He sat on a white wrought-iron chair in the shade of a broad tree with thick olive-green leaves, his long legs stretched almost lazily out in front of him, combat boots crossed at the ankles.

Shaka lay on the grass under his chair. In one hand Laroque held a white cup, the saucer resting on the glass-topped table. With his other, he ruffled his dog's fur.

It was an arresting vignette, an image for a magazine cover—the devastatingly handsome and powerful warlord at ease in his garden. A garden he'd *stolen,* she reminded herself, just as he'd stolen the whole damn country.

A king and his family had once lived here, a royal family that had mysteriously vanished from their Parisian home in exile just over a year ago.

It had been whispered that Le Diable and his French connections might even be responsible for the disappearance of King Desmond Douala and his wife and son, perhaps even their murder in Paris, before he'd come to take the country for himself.

She breathed in deeply, and began to walk over the lawn toward him, the grass springy under her feet. The morning sun was hot, the sound of birds riotous in the trees above. Shaka looked up as she approached, then glanced at his master for direction. The dog adored him, she noted. And he clearly loved his pet. It showed a human side to him, a capacity for care, for empathy.

From what Emily had learned about Laroque and his violent, transient lifestyle, Shaka might well be his *only* true friend in life. She wondered what he'd done for companionship before Shaka. As far as she knew the dog had only appeared on the scene with Laroque's arrival on that Spanish boat.

As she reached the table, she realized the sound that emanated from the tree above came not from birds, but from a troop of curious little monkeys that cavorted in the branches like naughty tufted gremlins.

Laroque stood the instant he saw her, his movement as fluid as a jaguar's. Emily guessed he was never truly at rest. He'd not have survived otherwise.

He held out his hand. "Take a seat," he said, motioning to the vacant chair. His eyes were lighter, somehow even less human in the stark sunlight. The juxtaposition against his smooth coffee-toned skin was truly startling.

He caught her staring. "I'm used to it," he said. "They're my father's eyes." A faint bitterness underscored his words. "That's why they call me Le Diable. Did you know that?"

Surprise rippled through her. "No. I…I thought—"

"You thought the moniker was a result of some terrible action of mine, didn't you?" He didn't give her a chance to answer. "Most assume the worst. Rumors grow legs of their own."

People want to believe in monsters.

She sat, momentarily self-conscious and trying to avoid the piercing green of his eyes. She could see that calling him Le Diable would have been a natural leap for the people of this continent. This was a place of animism and spirits and a powerful belief in dark magic, and while this man walked this territory with African blood and natural ease, he did so to his own drum. He was different in both looks and spirit, and that kind of independence always made people uneasy. It made them afraid.

But while Laroque had inherited his father's eyes and massive build, those strong Dutch genes were offset by his Ubasian mother's striking beauty and innate grace. He was an exotic blend of primal African charm, Germanic strength and a uniquely European finesse. He was a global man.

And the effect was totally captivating.

But Emily was more interested in what lay beneath the surface. She wanted to know how much more of his father was in him. She needed to know if this man would talk if captured and tortured.

He lifted a tall silver pot. "Coffee?"

The gesture, the question, was so simple, so normal. Yet it wasn't. She glanced up at his face, and was suddenly sideswiped by the fact she might be responsible for this man's death. "Thank you," she said, feeling guilty. "It smells divine."

"Ubasi grown and roasted," he said as he poured.

She watched the rich liquid stream from the spout, wondering how much of her discomfort stemmed from the fact that she was physically, and yes, even mentally, intrigued by him.

"What are you thinking?" he asked as he set the pot down.

Her eyes cut to his and she laughed lightly. "Men don't ask questions like that."

He smiled. "I'm not your average man."

He was right on that count. "I was thinking," she said reaching for the cream, "how badly I need a cup of coffee. You say it's local?"

"Grown in the foothills of the Purple Mountains." He settled back into his chair, hooking one boot over the other. "My dream is to see Ubasian coffee and cocoa exported around the world someday as a very exclusive fair-trade brand."

Another surprise. "Fair trade?"

He angled his head, studied her. "You did not expect this?"

"No, I mean, I have no reason not to. I just thought—"

"That I was a warmonger, after nothing but destruction and personal spoils?"

She snorted softly, unexpectedly amused, and sipped the coffee. Damned if it wasn't some of the finest she'd ever tasted. "It's good," she said. "Really good." There was something about this guy she was starting to really like.

The jolt of caffeine helped lift her spirits, too. "Shall we talk about interview parameters, or do you want to tell me your plans for the Ubasi economy first?"

His eyes narrowed. "I want to empower the people of my country, Emma," he said, watching her steadily. "If you've done your research, as I suspect you have, you'll know I was schooled by an assortment of Catholic nuns and priests at various missions across the continent, and that I obtained a masters in economics at the Sorbonne. I studied between my mercenary missions. I used the proceeds from my commissions to fund my studies, and to make investments, which have paid off very well."

Oh, she'd done her research, all right. Jean-Charles Laroque was not only a warrior, but a shrewd investor with a phenomenally solid portfolio of offshore holdings. He'd made war pay. Personally. By investing his spoils wisely. Yet here he was saying he'd overthrown Ubasi for the good of the people. It shouldn't surprise her.

A true tyrant often claimed to be acting in the name of "his" people, but Laroque would be the first to turn around and sacrifice those very same people to keep, or increase, his hold on power. And he'd crush any opposition with force.

Just as he would crush her if he found out who she really was. She had to remember that.

"You're an astute businessman, Your Excellency, as well as a guerrilla war expert and master strategist," she said, aiming to flatter as well as probe. "You clearly don't need the cash, but you still choose to fight. You must like it."

"I fight only for Ubasi," he said. "Once I have properly secured the country, that's it. I'm done."

"No more mercenary work?"

"No more."

Emily set her cup carefully into its saucer. "You're

telling me that Ubasi is somehow the pot at the end of your rainbow? That you've accrued enough oil wealth from this latest acquisition to set you up for life?"

"Those oil fields are mine in name only, Emma," he said quietly. "The wealth will go to the people."

"I don't understand."

"There's a lot you don't understand."

She feigned a smile. "Then we have much ground to cover, don't we?"

He gave a curt nod, reached for a platter of sliced fruit and handed it to her. "But first, you must eat."

The fruit was exotic and sinfully sweet. Emily wiped the juice from her chin with a napkin as a server materialized at their side with a basket of freshly baked French pastries. She studied the exchange between Laroque and his servant as the pastries were set on the table, detecting a genuine friendliness between the two.

Laroque's staff liked him, and from what she'd seen in the street yesterday, his subjects idolized him. Even more telling was the respect *he* showed his staff. This man was not at all what she'd expected. She filed this revelation with her other surprises.

"Tell me, Your Excellency," she said when the server departed, "why are doing this in Ubasi? You make it sound as though this place is some kind of endgame for you."

"It is," he said. "And you may call me Jean."

She nodded, a little nervous at the sharp flint in his eyes in spite of the step toward familiarity. She'd hit on something. She needed to keep probing, but the aggressive lines in his features warned her not to. She moistened her lips. "You're…making me think this is something you're prepared to die for, Jean."

He said nothing. His eyes narrowed to slits and a small muscle pulsed at the base of his jaw. Silence swelled with the rising temperatures. Even the monkeys had grown quiet.

"I am," he said suddenly.

Emily stopped chewing.

He leaned forward, his eyes sparking with cold green fire, a predatory danger crackling from his body. "Understand this, I will *not* go down without a fight…*Emma*."

The pastry in her mouth suddenly felt dry.

"And…that fight will be to the death?"

"I don't like losing. I plan to win. But I *will* die fighting if that's what it takes."

She didn't doubt him, not for a moment. His intent was as crystal clear as the green in his eyes.

So it was unlikely Jean-Charles Laroque would make a good prisoner. He'd probably give nothing under torture. And capture could make this man a martyr. She'd witnessed firsthand the elemental passion of his people—he was like some kind of god to them. Such was the manipulative power of a shrewd despot.

Taking Le Diable alive could potentially spark a civil war.

Assassination—death—might be the only answer.

The idea left her strangely deflated.

"It's for my sister," he said suddenly.

"I…beg your pardon?"

"My sister, Tamasha. She was a key political activist here in Ubasi. She opposed the Souleyman regime during his bloody eight-year reign. Tamasha's voice of dissent was growing strong, along with her support. She had a gift for mobilizing an oppressed people. So Souleyman silenced her. Just over a year ago." His eyes flicked away briefly, but not fast enough to hide a flare of raw anguish that made Emily's heart squeeze.

"He killed her children first, slit their throats like goats. He made her watch. Then he cut her throat, in front of her home. He made the people of her village watch that."

Emily was speechless.

"You didn't know I had a sister, did you?"

"No… No, I didn't."

"Neither did I. Not until two years ago. That's when…" The words died on his lips, a small twitch tugging at a corner of his control. He looked away again, longer this time. When he turned back, she could see the savage emotion in his eyes. Not helpless pain, but the kind of bitter and raw hurt that fuelled revenge.

For the first time Emily felt like she was actually *seeing* this man and not some mask. He'd just made himself vulnerable to her and the gesture filled her chest with inexplicable emotion.

He reached for his pocket, withdrew his wallet, flipped it open and slid a battered black-and-white photo over the table. Emily picked it up. "This is her?"

He dipped his head silently.

"God, she's beautiful, Jean. She looks so much like your mother, like *you.*"

A wry smile ghosted his lips. "She's pure Ubasian. Not a mongrel like me."

Her eyes shot to his. Is that how he saw himself? The impure son of a murderer and rapist, not a true African?

Something close to compassion unfurled inside her.

He pocketed the photo quickly, as if he'd made a mistake even showing her. "Can you imagine that?" he said, his mouth curling into a harsh smile. "The infamous Diable actually had family—a real sister, nieces, nephews." He leaned forward sharply. "Do know what that was like, Emma? To *discover* that? His eyes narrowed and his voice turned husky. "Souleyman took that from me. He took my family. He murdered them before I could ever meet them." His voice grew dangerously quiet. "It was a mistake not to kill him when I could, because now he's coming back for more. He's growing strong again. But this time I *will* end his life."

She had an impulse to touch him, to ease his spirit. She lifted her hand almost reflexively, caught herself and ran it through her hair instead.

He noticed the gesture, her indecision. His eyes connected with hers, and the air felt suddenly charged. It wasn't only the chemistry that had shifted between them, they'd connected on some deeper level. Emily felt as if she was at a critical turning point, unsure which way to go.

To her relief, she saw one of his guards hastening down the lawn, but relief segued into mild alarm when Laroque stiffened sharply at the sight of his soldier.

He launched to his feet, long strides taking him swiftly over the lawn to meet his man out of her earshot. Their exchange was urgent, conducted in low tones she couldn't pick up.

When he returned to the table his features were once again impenetrable. He held his hand out to her. "Come, I have something to show you."

"What?"

"My sister's village."

Nerves skittered through her chest. "Why?" She glanced toward the retreating militia guy. "Is…is there some kind of trouble?"

"There's been a skirmish near the palace," he said. "Some of Souleyman's insurgents have infiltrated deeper into Ubasi. They're getting closer to the capital. My men have subdued them, but there may be more. I cannot leave you here alone, and I must speak to the headman of Tamasha's village. I owe him a visit, and I need his help. He needs to prepare his people for battle, protect the women and children, and he must send out alerts to other rural settlements. I'm taking reinforcements to him."

He waited, hand held out, rock steady.

Emily stared at his hand, confusion tightening

inside her. She needed to talk to Jacques, tell him things were not what they seemed in Ubasi.

Maybe if she stayed behind at the castle, she could find a way to communicate while Laroque was gone. "I think I'd rather remain here while—"

His brows lowered sharply. "It's for *your* safety."

"I…I'm prepared to take the risk, thanks, Jean. I'm tired after—"

"We have a deal, Emma," he said very quietly. "Don't we?"

She studied the hard planes of his face, marveling at how different he'd looked in those few moments he dropped his guard. He could be manipulating her, working up her empathy, sucking her in with charismatic charm. Or he could be telling the truth.

Either way, she was trapped. The only way out was to see this mission through, knowing that any misstep might cost her.

"Yes," she said softly, placing her hand in his. "We have a deal."

His fingers closed firmly around hers as he lifted her to her feet. He didn't release her right away, and she didn't pull back, either.

Laroque looked deep into Emma's eyes, searching for some hint of truth. What he felt was desire. Unbidden and sharp. He felt himself swell with need as he held her hand, her skin so soft in his rough palm. His breathing quickened. Her scent was intoxicating. Everything about her was arousing. He could see she felt it, too. He could read it in her eyes. And in this moment, as he held her close, Jean knew he'd do whatever it took to sleep with her.

Enemy or not.

And if she *was* a spy? Well, then, she was equipped for the game. She knew what she was in for. She knew his reputation, and thus her chances.

But was *he* equipped to deal with her if she turned out to be a traitor? Something in her eyes warned him he wasn't.

Chapter 5

Jacques Sauvage hung up the telephone, deep in thought. According to the Geographic International team leader, Max Rutger, Emily Carlin was inside Le Diable's fortress voluntarily. GPS confirmed her laptop and phone were there. So why wasn't she using them?

He leaned back in his chair. Carlin hadn't been active in the field for some time, but he was confident in the training he gave *all* his contractors. If they wished to remain on FDS books, they were compelled to do a refresher boot camp annually, regardless of whether there was work available. Emily was no exception. He had to trust her. If she was in trouble, she'd have sent a coded message.

Still, if for some reason she failed to make contact

by midnight Thursday, Jacques's men would move on the palace regardless, extract Emily, and eliminate Le Diable. This was the backup plan. CIA director Blake Weston had insisted on it.

Ideally, Souleyman's insurgents would be the ones to carry out the actual assassination. The FDS would simply arm and position them.

Jacques's operatives had already made contact with Souleyman's camp east of the Ubasi border, and they'd found Souleyman to have a surprisingly healthy opposition force and network of spies already active inside Ubasi. He was planning a coup of his own. This made the FDS job incredibly simple.

Still, little things troubled Jacques. The source of Souleyman's weaponry and funding was, as yet, a mystery. He clearly had a rich source of income. The men he was hiring to retake Ubasi were not local.

And then there were the five hostages, taken by Laroque's rebels from Nigeria. There was still no official claim of responsibility for their capture, nor any ransom demand.

This was unusual, especially given the fact three of the hostages were American citizens. Things were just too damn quiet on that score. Not even Weston seemed overly concerned.

If Jacques were in Weston's shoes, he'd want answers on that front ASAP. But his job was not to second-guess the policy or strategy of his employer, in this case the United States of America.

Nevertheless, Jacques was having the backgrounds of those five hostages checked for himself. He liked to have *all* his bases covered. He liked his questions answered, and right now things were not quite adding up.

12:00 Zulu. Saturday, November 9.
Northwest of Basaroutou

They traveled in convoy, armed men standing in the backs of Jeeps scanning walls of dense foliage that encroached on either side of their vehicles with a keenness that unnerved Emily.

The sun was at its zenith, white-hot and small in a hazy sky. As the temperature peaked, the humidity began to press down on them, leaching color and clarity from the landscape. They'd been traveling for more than two hours. Emily's throat felt dry, and her body was drenched in perspiration.

Shaka sat between her and Laroque on the backseat of one of the Jeeps, panting hard, his black fur glistening in the sun. The dog was growing accustomed to her, and Emily was grateful for the buffer against Laroque's body. Her physical reaction to his touch in the garden had alarmed her. It was that potent.

She pet Shaka's head. "He's thirsty."

Laroque's eyes remained locked on to the dark green tangle of jungle, his muscles tense. "It'll have to wait. Can't stop now."

"You're worried about an ambush, aren't you?"

He grunted, which didn't ease her nerves.

"Do you have some kind of intelligence alerting you to the possibility?"

His eyes shot suddenly to hers, held her gaze. Christ, she'd have to watch herself. He was highly suspicious, as if waiting for her to make a mistake. She had no idea how much of her story he believed.

"He's a great dog," she said, trying to shift focus. "You're really fond of him, aren't you?"

"You can trust dogs," Laroque said tonelessly, turning once again to face the jungle.

"Where'd you get him?" she asked, trying to hold back the hair flapping around her face.

"Senegal. He was a stray on the docks where we stopped to collect a weapons cache."

"So you just took him in out of the goodness of your heart, while out shopping for black-market weapons?"

He snorted without looking at her. "No. He was the right color."

"Oh well, *that* explains it."

The convoy slowed to an easier pace more in keeping with the abysmal road conditions. The danger, whatever it was, must have passed. Laroque's body relaxed somewhat, too. He turned to her, but he didn't smile.

"This is a complex land, Emma, steeped in voodoo tradition and magic. People follow a different set of beliefs. When Souleyman took power, the Ubasi high priestess issued a prophecy. She decreed that Souleyman would remain leader until a man with demon eyes and a black spirit-dog came to destroy him." He paused, watching her carefully. "And do you know what Souleyman did? He ordered every black dog in Ubasi shot on sight. That was eight years ago."

"So you purposefully taunted him with the prophecy by bringing a black dog with you?"

"No. I simply made it come true. Like I told you, Emma, what is fact is far less important than what is believed, especially in this part of the world. Souleyman believed the high priestess. So did his men. So did the people of Ubasi. I brought Shaka with me as a tool to crush him psychologically."

"And your eyes—"

"They sealed the deal."

"That prophecy could be interpreted a hundred ways, Jean."

"Yes, but when Souleyman got word that a man with 'devil eyes' had sailed into port with a black dog at his side, and that he'd come with men and guns, he was instantly psychologically defeated. He panicked. His men fled in terror. His army was in disarray as it was—most of his soldiers hadn't seen stipends in more than six months. They had no intention of dying for a man who'd already given up."

"So *that's* how you managed to overthrow an entire kingdom in a few hours without killing a single person."

"Strategy can be more powerful than the sword. You have to get a man at his own game." He tapped his temple. "A game of the mind."

She swallowed. "So…Souleyman just gave up and surrendered?"

"Like a pathetic bastard."

"Smart," she said, and looked away. That's exactly how her ex had gotten her—a game of the mind.

Was that what Laroque was doing now, playing her at her own game? She wasn't sure what to trust anymore.

"No, not so smart," he said suddenly. "I should have slit his throat, done it right there as he surrendered. My mistake has allowed him to regroup and come back for me, for Ubasi."

Emily shot a look at him, and saw a moment of pure hatred in his face.

"Why didn't you kill him?"

"I have no taste for cold-blooded execution. I fight a man on equal terms, not one who lies whimpering at my feet." His jaw tightened. "But I've learned my lesson."

"It's strange, Jean, don't you think, how a stray black dog just sort of happened to be waiting for you at those docks in Senegal?"

"Don't read too much into these things, Emma. If you think too much about them you give them power, they become real."

She laughed, but inside she felt murky, strange, off center. "You don't believe in that voodoo stuff yourself, do you?"

"My people do. That alone makes it something I

have to work with. One cannot ignore the influence of voodoo and magic in local politics."

She studied the arrogant lines of his face. Laroque was clearly a master at propaganda. He'd managed to portray himself as Ubasi's rightful leader by linking himself to the high priestess's prophecy and thus aligning himself with the country's most popular religion, almost shaping himself into its cult figurehead. His dog was a tool, part of the image. It was classic tyrannical behavior.

"But you *do* love your dog?"

He cocked a brow in surprise. "Shaka?" he said, touching the animal's head. "He's my one friend."

She believed him.

The stray may have initially been a strategic tool, but Shaka had become much more to Laroque. The man did have a soul, of that Emily was becoming certain, but even tyrants had soft spots in their hearts. Weak spots.

She watched his hand resting protectively on Shaka's head, and for a brief moment wondered how it might feel to have his protective touch on her. Her cheeks went hot and she glanced away quickly, shocked with herself.

It was just an atavistic female reaction, she told herself. But she was lying. It was even more simple. *She'd* been specifically wired to go for men like him. Just as her mother had been.

And look what had happened to her.

Their Jeep swerved suddenly to avoid a small

yellow monkey that scampered into the road with a baby clutched to her back.

Emily gasped, grabbing the side as their vehicle jolted into a ditch and kicked up a cloud of sand as it accelerated and fishtailed back onto the road. Her heart skittered wildly.

She tried to catch her breath, not sure what had rattled her more—the near accident, or the realization she was becoming dangerously attracted to Laroque.

As they drove by the small primate sat up and bared her teeth, screeching at them in a high-pitched staccato, her small eyes wild.

Emily's heart thudded as their convoy began a descent into a lower plateau knotted with tropical growth. The air trapped in the hollow of land was intensely close. Trees grew taller, forest giants punching high up out of the canopy. Moisture dripped.

Two vultures circled up high on hot currents of air. Emily watched the birds, unable to get the sound of the monkey's screech out of her mind. She felt as though Laroque was taking her deep into an untamed place where strange magic seemed all too possible.

The village was nestled into a red valley alongside a twisting chocolate-brown river. As they negotiated the dirt track down into the lowlands, Emily could make out thatched wattle-and-daub huts painted with bright colors clustered in groups around a central well. Crop gardens had been cut back into the jungle, and the scent of cooking and wood fires tinged the humid air.

She felt she was journeying back in time.

Their convoy rumbled into the encampment with a town crier heralding their arrival on an ancient loud-hailer. People began to emerge from the gardens and huts—men with the physiques of hunters carrying ceremonial spears and shields, women wrapped in brightly colored swaths of fabric, some with babies strapped to their backs, and elders with bent bodies, hair white as hoarfrost against dark skin.

Barefoot children with bony little bodies in ragged clothes scampered ahead of the adults to greet the visitors, smiles wide and bright. A few emaciated curs joined the excitement with yelps of encouragement. Emily's heart did a tight little tumble.

"Your sister lived *here?*" she whispered as she watched the timeless scene unfolding in front of her, not knowing why she kept her voice low. Perhaps it was because speaking out loud might pop the fragile spell the village had woven around her. Perhaps she instinctively felt that some sort of deference was required.

He pointed to a thatched hut on the outskirts of the encampment. It was painted with green-and-orange patterns, small windows hewn into mud walls. "That was her home."

Where she'd been killed.

Emily swallowed.

She hadn't expected *this* when he'd said Tamasha had been a political activist. She wasn't sure what exactly she'd expected.

Their convoy slowed to a halt in the town center and the townsfolk converged on them.

Laroque's soldiers shook hands and joked with the men as cigarettes were passed around. The children crowded around the Jeeps trying to touch everything—children like Tamasha's, thought Emily. Innocent smiling faces just like these had been slaughtered by Souleyman's men while she'd been forced to watch. While this whole village had been forced to watch. Emily's throat grew tight and her eyes burned unexpectedly.

She tried to shake the disturbing image, and became aware that Laroque was watching her.

"You all right?"

"I…did Tamasha have a man in her life?" She *needed* to know if their father was among the faces that greeted them.

"He was killed by Souleyman's men a few weeks after their youngest child was born," Laroque said, his voice strangely tender in a way she hadn't heard before. "It's what made Tamasha so angry. She channeled her grief into fighting for a democratic Ubasi, free of Souleyman. She began to travel from village to village on that small motorbike over there—" he pointed to a rusty old scooter resting against the wall of Tamasha's hut "—to spread her ideas."

He clasped her hand, helping her out of the Jeep. "There's no other form of communication between the villages apart from travelers and word-of-mouth."

She looked up into Laroque's face. "She was like you, Jean."

His brow lifted in question.

"She was a fighter. A person who physically needed to fix what was broken." *You also fuel your actions with grief. You won't allow yourself to heal, to let her death go. You want to "fix" it instead, with bare hands and guns.*

"You want revenge," she added.

"Justice," he answered.

"It's the same thing, really."

His eyes held hers for a beat, then he moved sharply away. "Come, I'll introduce you to everyone, then I must talk to the men and tell them how to prepare."

Emily watched the children scampering alongside Laroque as he crossed the village square ahead of her. He touched the head of each child in acknowledgement, then he stooped suddenly to pick up a little girl. He raised her high up onto his shoulders, and she shrieked with laughter as he swooped back down to catch the hand of another very small barefooted boy.

Laroque laughed with them as he walked, a warm and elemental sound that caught Emily right in the gut. She noted with mild shock that the notorious Diable was totally free here, in this village. It was home to him. It was his symbolic heart of Ubasi—it defined the country's people, the traditional lifestyles, the purity of his continent.

That's why he'd come personally to talk to the

headman, and that's why he was bringing militia to protect them. He wanted to protect his home. Emotion rose like a warm tide through her chest, and with it came a very real sense of affection for this enigmatic man.

She tried to remind herself that Jean-Charles Laroque was a tyrant. His rule here wasn't legal. It wasn't ethical. But somehow, being here, seeing it all with her own eyes—and beginning to understand *why* he'd done it—it just didn't seem wrong. And in that moment, Emily's trusted moral compass no longer read true.

She suddenly wanted no part of a coup that would attack this lifestyle—these people. Their ideals. Their dreams. Her throat tasted bitter, dry.

She was more trapped than she'd realized.

Chapter 6

Laroque exited the hut with the men, Shaka at his heels, and stilled as he caught sight of her.

Emma was at the well, surrounded by a group of women and children all giggling hysterically as she tried to walk without dislodging the bucket of water she had balanced on her head. A bolt of bright turquoise fabric with yellow squares had been wrapped over her T-shirt and khaki pants, restraining her movements, and tears of laugher poured down her cheeks.

She saw him looking, and froze.

The bucket fell to the ground with a dull thud and rolled over the packed red earth, spilling water that darkened the ochre soil to the color of blood. Everyone fell quiet for a moment. Just the raucous call of birds and a handful of small monkeys chattering in branches above filled the afternoon.

Silently he approached her and placed his hand proprietarily at her waist. "That color brings out your eyes," he said in a whisper. "But it's supposed to be worn without the regular clothes underneath."

Her cheeks flushed, and she quickly began to unravel the wrap.

A frisson of heat chased up his spine at her reaction. Laughter made her beautiful, blushing even more so. It showed a softness she tried to hide. It made her look incredibly feminine, and even more desirable to him.

Seeing her wrapped in traditional Ubasi dress, right here in Tamasha's village, laughing with *his* people, was dangerously provocative to him. For the first time in his life Laroque wondered what it might be like to take a wife and build a home, in this country. The thought shocked him to his foundations.

His heart began to beat boldly as he watched Emma hastily rolling up her bolt of fabric, as if trying to bundle up her embarrassment. She tucked it firmly under her arm, straightened her back, and looked him coolly in the eye. "It's a gift," she said, jutting her chin toward the fabric. "They were showing me how to wear it."

"And the bucket?" He was toying with her now; he couldn't help it any more than a cat could restrain itself from chasing a mouse.

Uncertainty washed back into her eyes. He

smiled, again unable to help it. He liked her this way. Natural. No games.

He knew he had to be careful with her. Her sophisticated equipment was suspicious, as was the timing of her presence in the country. But right now all he wanted was for her to be who she claimed she was. All he wanted was to touch her.

And he did.

He placed his hand at the base of her spine, and she inhaled softly as he did. He guided her with subtle pressure from hut to hut as he greeted each family individually, introducing her by name, Shaka obediently following at their heels.

She felt good under his hands. He enjoyed the sense of ownership as he escorted her through the small town. And he liked the way she was coyly avoiding his eyes. She wanted him. He could tell. And it made him feel good.

They came to the humble abode his sister had called home. Laroque dropped his hand and motioned for the others to leave them alone for a moment.

They didn't enter Tamasha's dwelling. He couldn't.

"It's remained empty all this time?" she asked, meeting his eyes with a new openness.

He nodded, replacing his black shades, distancing himself from the genuine empathy he saw in her face. Sympathy made him edgy.

"Tell me about her, Jean," she said gently. "How did you finally learn of her existence? Why did it take so long?"

He inhaled deeply, wondering how much of himself he should expose to her. The silence between them grew thick, but not uncomfortable. The jungle wrapped its sultry-afternoon cloak around them and palm fronds rattled as birds moved through leaves, pecking at fruit. He reached down to touch Shaka and ruffled the dog's fur, drawing strength from the connection.

"Tamasha's birth was my mother's darkest secret, Emma, and she died keeping it." Laroque stared at the small, brightly painted hut. "My mother had an affair with a cousin of the king's family while visiting her Ubasi homeland, and she returned to give birth to her in this village, in secret, while my father was on an extended contract. My father had begun to change, you see, and my mother had grown very afraid of him. Too afraid to leave him. She believed that if Peter Laroque had discovered her affair, he'd have killed both her and Tamasha." He paused, his chest feeling oddly tight. "She made Tamasha promise she would *never* make contact with the family—including me, her brother—while my father was still alive."

"Was Tamasha older or younger than you?"

His mouth twisted in a grim smile. "She was my kid sister, two years younger."

"So she'd have been eleven when your mother died?"

His eyes whipped to hers, tension returning to his body as he recalled the photo she had in her computer. This woman knew too much about him.

"I did my research on you, Jean," she said softly. "I've seen the famous photo of you being dragged at age thirteen from the hospital bed of your dying mother."

It was as if she was reading his mind. He didn't like it. The silence grew charged.

"It must have been tough," she said.

"I never saw my mother alive again after that photo was taken," he said. "My father took me straight into the battlefields of Africa, where he taught me how to be a soldier."

"Who raised Tamasha?"

"Guardians. They instilled in her the importance of keeping the promise after my mother died, and when Tamasha grew older, she came to hear herself about the exploits of Peter Laroque. At that stage he was already rumored to have turned murderous. Criminal. Tamasha knew our mother was right, that he was an incredibly brutal man, and that there was a good chance he would hurt her. And later, of course, she wanted to protect her own children."

He paused, turned to look into her eyes. There was a directness in her gaze, and a compassion that made him uncomfortable. He looked away. "Because of my father's predisposition for violence, I remained estranged from my sister. And because I was in his custody and forced to fight under him from the age of thirteen, people assume I am like him. But I'm not. No one understood my relationship to him. No one knew me at all."

Even now.

"He was all you had, Jean," she offered. "You depended on him."

Laroque was quiet for a moment. "I *hated* him."

"You must have witnessed the most abysmal atrocities as a kid."

"I wasn't much different from many children on this continent. I didn't have a choice."

"When did you leave him?"

"When…" He hesitated. No. He wasn't going to tell her about that night. "The last time I saw him I was twenty."

"So when your dad was killed in that Congo raid almost two years ago, that was when Tamasha finally contacted you?"

"She got a letter to me in Paris."

Laroque wasn't going to tell Emma, either, that his politically active sister had made contact with him via King Douala, who'd been living in innocuous exile in Paris for the past eight years. The king's role in this Ubasi mission had to remain secret, for the royal family's protection.

Laroque's men had taken King Desmond Douala and his wife and son into hiding in rural Spain before mounting the coup. No one could know where the royal family was sequestered until Ubasi had been stabilized enough for their return. After living in France for eight long, unhappy years, Douala was aging, unwell. He'd wanted one last chance to reclaim his country from the hands of Souleyman. He wanted democracy, and he wanted his young son at the helm of the process. He'd paid Laroque handsomely in oil concessions to overthrow Souleyman and take back Ubasi. Laroque's brief from the king was now to establish a police force and strong military presence, so that it would be safe to bring back his son.

Laroque had initially refused the contract. There was no way he was going to masquerade as some tyrant until the king's rightful return. But then Douala had shown him the letter from Tamasha, a sister he never knew he had, the sister who'd followed *his* life, biding her time.

Tamasha had believed her brother ideal for the role of reclaiming the throne. She'd convinced the king of it. And she'd believed Laroque would do it because he had Ubasi blood.

Seeing that letter had changed the entire direction of Laroque's life in that one instant. He actually had family, a place he might belong, even call *home*.

He took the commission and began to prepare for war.

Then news came of her death. At Souleyman's hand.

The instant that news had reached him, the Ubasi mission became an all-consuming personal obsession for Laroque. He would succeed—or die trying.

And now, just as things were finally looking promising for the king's return, the CIA agents had turned up dead. The hostages had been taken from Nigeria. Souleyman had mysteriously grown in power.

And Emma had appeared on his doorstep.

Her voice broke through the silence. "But you never got to meet her?"

"No."

Emma reached out and placed her hand on the bare skin of his arm. Her eyes, so damn wide and luminous, met his. Eyes that were the exact same color as dawn breaking over the Purple Mountains.

Laroque sat in stony silence as their convoy negotiated the rutted track on their return. The sky was turning a dusky twilight that made visibility a challenge as his eyes adjusted to the gray zone between day and night. The air was thick and heavy with a sense of foreboding.

He stole another look at Emma Sanford. Not only had this woman managed to get into his castle, she was getting right inside his head, poking into his secrets. She was also aiming at some vague area around his heart. She was forcing him to *feel*. Worse, she was making him talk.

He'd overstepped the mark. He needed to be more vigilant until he knew exactly what he was up against.

An explosion suddenly split the air, and their Jeep lurched violently sideways. A hot whoosh rushed past Laroque's face. It happened so fast he barely saw the next one coming.

Another explosion ripped through the jungle as a second vehicle hit a land mine. He saw the Jeep up ahead buck into the air, hood flying up, pieces of the vehicle separating in a spinning blur of red soil and twisted metal. The Jeep flipped, landing on its back, wheels helplessly spinning. Black smoke billowed, the scent of fire was acrid.

The convoy screeched to a halt, soldiers yelling and diving for cover as machine gun fire peppered the air.

Bullets thudded into metal and barked into the dirt road in puffs of dust.

Laroque's first instinct was to protect Emma. He threw himself over her as he reached for his holstered weapon. Shielding her, he aimed up into the tree that hung low over the road, the source of the gunfire. And he returned fire with staccato precision.

Whoever was in that tree immediately turned fire directly on him. He felt Emma's body jerk and shudder sharply under his as she gasped. Laroque felt hot blood on his arm. His stomach tightened and his vision turned scarlet with rage. *She'd been hit!*

In a rage, he reared up, oblivious to his own safety, and fired into the tree, again and again and again.

He hit his mark, and the sniper tumbled out from the low branches. His body glanced off the side of a Jeep, thudding into the dirt with a bounce. Laroque's men scrambled up out of the ditches and converged on him.

Laroque grabbed Emma's shoulders, pulled her up and turned her to face him.

Her eyes were wide, her face pale against the blood that soaked her shirt.

Chapter 7

"Shaka's been hit! Quick, Jean, help me!" Emily pulled herself free from Jean's grip. "I need something to stop the bleeding!" She pressed her hands over a wound on the dog's neck as blood welled dark through her pale fingers.

Alarm flared in Laroque's eyes, then darkened to rage. He shot a quick look at his men, calculating casualties, assessing the status of the situation. Then he yelled something at her as he reached under the backseat of the Jeep, but Emily couldn't hear him. She was deaf, her ears still zinging from the explosions.

He yanked out a first-aid kit, flipped it open and pulled out a wad of bandages, urgency fueling his actions. He moved his mouth again. She shook her head. "I can't hear you!" she yelled.

He took her bloodied hand, pressed a roll of bandage against her palm, and closed her fingers over it. His eyes said it all: *Look after Shaka.*

The responsibility suddenly felt enormous. "Go!" she screamed. "Look after your men!"

He touched her shoulder briefly, then he was gone.

Emily quickly fingered through Shaka's bloody fur, her FDS first aid training skills kicking in. She could ascertain two wounds—a shot in the shoulder and one in the neck. He was losing blood fast. His eyes were rolling back and his mouth lolled open. His pulse was thready. Emily pressed the bandages firmly against the wounds, and glanced up. The dog was going to need proper medical attention, fast.

The scene she saw was apocalyptic. Acrid black smoke hung low over the burning and twisted vehicles. The battered bodies of two soldiers were strewn near the first Jeep that had hit the mine. Some of Laroque's men were scrambling to help injured comrades, others converged on the captive he'd shot from the tree, beating him as he writhed in pain.

Laroque pulled back his guards and jerked the captive up to his knees by the collar of his shirt. The sniper had been shot badly in the shoulder, and his shirt was bloody. Even from here Emily could see the stark whites of his terrified eyes against his dark skin.

Laroque demanded something, but the captive spat into his face.

Laroque stiffened with predatory anger, questioned the sniper again.

The man just stared up at him, breathing hard.

Laroque repeated his question.

The man winced as blood seeped from his shoulder, but still he didn't respond.

Laroque barked an order to his men and spun away as they dragged the captive into the jungle.

Emily heard a single gunshot, and bile rose in her throat.

Without missing a beat, Laroque strode toward her. Her heart kicked into overdrive and her stomach heaved as she tried to swallow the bitter taste in her mouth.

Not once did his eyes break contact with hers as his long legs ate the distance to the Jeep. And what she saw in those eyes frightened her.

She saw his father.

Emily forced herself to tear away from his lethal stare and quickly focused her attention on Shaka.

Laroque swung into the vehicle. *"Allez!"* he yelled to his driver as he pushed Emily's hands away from his dog and took Shaka gently into his lap.

He felt for the wounds himself, moving with experienced and fluid efficiency to staunch the bleeding.

The Jeep barked sideways out of the dust, and swerved around the carnage.

"You had him killed!" she yelled over the engine.

He looked up with eyes as flat and cold as a shark. "That sniper was one of my men," he said tonelessly.

"A soldier turned traitor. Working for Souleyman. Against my people."

In that moment Emily knew he would crush her if he ever discovered she was threatening what he held dear. This man operated on a take-no-prisoners basis, at least since he'd allowed Souleyman to escape. He clearly was not going to make that "mistake" again.

She wiped the perspiration from her forehead with the back of her wrist, before realizing all she was doing was transferring a gritty paste of blood and dust from one side of her face to the other, and suddenly she felt exhausted.

She stared at the dull green of jungle blurring by as they hit the ruts in the road at ridiculous speed, her teeth jarring with the impact.

Over the years events had taken an innocent young boy and shaped him into a brutal cold-blooded man with a dream he would now kill for.

And die for.

Just how far, she wondered, would Le Diable go if no one stopped him?

Would he really rest if he achieved his goal? Or would he take it to the next level, aiming higher, growing harder, hungrier, colder, bolstered by each success, fueled by each betrayal—a true tyrant on the rise?

Was it her job to stop him?

Or save him?

Was it even possible to alter the life course of a man like this once he was set in his tracks?

She closed her eyes, no longer even bothering to try to brace against the bone-jarring movement of the vehicle. She wasn't sure what her role in life was anymore. Yes, she was a profiler, but she was also a healer of broken minds.

In her previous FDS jobs she'd always maintained her objectivity. She'd always stayed removed from her subject. She'd always felt *right*.

Now she felt everything but.

21:48 Zulu. Saturday, November 9.
Ubasi Palace dining hall

The guards held back the doors, and Laroque swept into the dining hall, adrenaline pounding through his blood, making him rough, edgy. Frustrated.

Shaka's life was out of his hands. Whether or not his dog lived or died tonight was not in his command.

He stood still, steadying his breath as the double doors swung solidly shut behind him.

The long dining table had been set with white linen, candles, sparkling crystal and shimmering silverware. Emma stood next to the buffet at the far end of the room, her back to him. She wore a simple sleeveless black sheath that fell to her calves and molded to her figure in a way that made him think of sex. Her dark hair had been scooped back into a high ponytail. Functional. Undecorated. Elegant. And totally arresting.

She whirled round as he entered, and he saw what she was holding in her hands—his special photograph.

He walked slowly over to the buffet, his eyes holding hers as he drew closer, his stomach tightening with each step, his restless adrenaline spiking. He carefully took the framed photograph out of her hands and set it firmly back on the buffet.

He wanted it away from her.

He wanted distance between this seductive woman and that very deeply personal part of himself, that part of himself he kept on trying to find, and was losing tonight, perhaps in his dog.

"Is…is Shaka okay, Jean?" she asked softly.

There was that empathy in her violet eyes again—a genuine caring, a sense of something so incredibly personal.

He didn't want that.

He wanted to be back in charge.

"I had an army doctor check him. The bullets have been removed." His voice didn't feel right. "Shaka is stable, and sedated. If he survives the night, he'll stand a fair chance. The doctor is with him now." He hesitated. "There's…nothing more I can do."

She touched his arm. "I'm so sorry, Jean."

He glared at her hand, emotion tugging sharply at his mouth. He withdrew from her touch. "I know it's late," he said. "But I hope you will dine with me."

He should've eaten alone. But as much as he needed to feel in charge, he also couldn't be alone right now. He needed something he couldn't define—company, a connection. He wasn't the hell sure what he needed.

"Of course," she said, but she didn't move toward

the table. She was watching him with that all-knowing analytic gaze, and he knew she had to be thinking about what he had done today, about the traitor who had been killed.

"Look," he said. "I'm really sorry you had to see what you did."

"Was it necessary, Jean?"

He felt his energy darken. "I'm not in the mood for psychological games, Emma. He was one of *my* soldiers. He betrayed not just me, but my people, *my country*. He's been living under *my* roof while feeding information to my enemy's camp. I got wind of this from the captives apprehended during the skirmish this morning. That's why we took extra precaution on the way to Tamasha's village. Clearly it wasn't enough."

"He didn't have to die like that."

Irritation darted down his chest. "I don't need your approval." He held his arm out, sorry now that he'd asked her to join him. "Let's eat."

Her eyes flicked to the grandfather clock, as if she didn't have the luxury of time. "That old black-and-white photograph," she said, indicating the silver frame he'd just replaced. "That's your father, isn't it? With you and your mom. You look about five years old in that picture."

He lowered his arm slowly, feeling the pressure building inside him. He said nothing.

She gave him a measured look. "I didn't expect you to have a photo of Peter Laroque on display."

His heart pumped harder, but he remained silent.

"You kept it because it was taken when you were still a genuine family, didn't you? It represents a time when there was still hope and promise in your life, before things went wrong."

He snapped. "*Enough,* Emma!"

Her eyes narrowed sharply. Then she nodded. "I'm sorry, Jean. I don't mean to push. I…it's…it's just that I'm not sure how much time I'm going to have with you…for the book, given all that's happening in Ubasi." She took his arm, drawing him closer. "Come, why don't we eat?"

Conflict churned dangerously low and hot in his gut, and the cool touch of her skin against his unfurled ribbons of something dark and hungry inside him.

Tonight he needed someone.

Damn, he needed *her.* All of her.

He pulled out her chair for her, steeling himself against her scent as she seated herself.

He took his place at the head of the table, flipped open his napkin, laid it on his lap and lifted the silver domes off the dishes. He poured wine and they ate in awkward silence. When the chink of cutlery grew too annoying, he slammed his knife and fork down and looked up. "He killed her," he said. Then cursed himself for having said anything at all.

Emma's eyes flickered, a quick sweep of long dark lashes over buttermilk skin. "What did you say?"

"My father killed my mother."

"I…I thought your mother died of a recreational drug overdose, after several years of abuse." She faltered a little, clearly worrying that she was over-stepping her mark. "I…it was in the tabloid archives I studied before coming here, Jean." He heard the hint of apology in her voice.

He reached for his glass, took a deep sip of wine. "Peter Laroque introduced my mother to the drugs that killed her. My mother may have been beautiful and famous, but she was also emotionally fragile, and very dependent on her man."

Emma's mouth tightened and a strange look crept into her eyes. She set down her knife and fork as if she'd suddenly lost her appetite.

"The drugs he gave her were highly addictive," he said. "He had to have known they would destroy her."

"Why did he do it?" She almost whispered the words, a look of growing recognition in her eyes that piqued Laroque's curiosity.

"He was an insanely jealous man, Emma. He loved my mother's beauty and he loved the fame and money that came with it, yet he resented the atten-tion it got her, especially from other men."

She reached for her wineglass, took a swig, and when she set her glass down he noticed her hands were shaking. Laroque frowned inwardly.

"Peter Laroque needed a woman who wouldn't stop him from going away to fight," he said. "Yet while he was away he'd torture himself imagining his wife having affairs. He'd grow increasingly wild with jealousy until he'd come home to claim her physically, roughly. He wanted both his freedom and total domination of his woman. He couldn't seem to reconcile these two overriding desires." He paused, thinking. "It was as if he needed to sabotage her. My father grew increasingly paranoid, more destructive, and each time he came home…he'd take her more violently."

"You *witnessed* this?"

"Yes."

Intensity darkened her eyes. "Why didn't she leave him?"

"She *couldn't*. She was afraid of him, and at the same time strangely dependent on him. He could be a very compelling man."

Emma's breathing grew slightly ragged. Her eyes flicked toward the open French doors, as if she were seeking some sort of mental escape of her own.

Intrigued, Laroque held up the bottle of cabernet. "More wine?"

She nodded, too quickly, and he poured.

He filled his own glass. "It got to a point where my father would leave her a supply of drugs each time he went on another commission, as if he wanted her to blot herself out until he returned, as though he couldn't bear her actually having a life without him."

"It was his way of locking her up while he was gone," she said, her voice hoarse.

Laroque nodded, watching her eyes. "And he always

came back with more drugs. He was a sick man, Emma, and his demons grew more violent with time."

She paled visibly. "Why did he take *you* away? Why didn't he just leave you be?"

He snorted. "My mother was dying. He had another contract to fulfill, and he knew that if she died while he was away, the authorities might step in, and he'd risk losing me. In his own very sick way, he loved his son, he loved the fact that he even had one. It appealed to the male in him." Laroque leaned forward. "And you know what, Emma? As much as I *hated* him, as much as I blamed him for my mother's death, and for taking me away before I could say goodbye to her, I came to *need* him. Especially in those early years."

"That's perfectly understandable," she said, almost too quickly, her voice too light. "You were a child, totally alone in a foreign world, of *course* you needed him."

He shrugged. "I needed his approval, and that makes me sick to my stomach now. I endured the blood, the violence, and I fought alongside my father, because he *was* my father, because I wanted his praise, and…he was all I had." Emotion heated his eyes. "And because I was angry. I fought because I was angry. I hurt people, because of *him.*"

She swore bitterly, turning her face away.

"Emma?"

She took a moment. When she turned back to face him, he could read distress in her eyes.

He placed his hand over hers. "Have I…I'm sorry if I have upset you."

She shook her head. "No…no, I'm fine. I was…" She inhaled sharply. "I was just thinking about family."

He studied her face. It bothered him that he knew nothing about her. Not once had she mentioned anything about her own past or her own family. His suspicions simmered back to the surface.

"What about you, Emma? What does your father do? Where is *your* mother?"

Her eyes shuttered. She wiped her mouth with her napkin. "I have a boring academic life, Jean," she said. "Besides, this interview is about you."

He picked up his knife and fork and cut into his meat, but from the corner of his eye he saw her take another deep swig of wine. She was trying to take the edge off something, and it deepened his curiosity.

"Tell me about the oil in Ubasi, Jean," she said, setting her glass down too carefully.

Laroque lifted his eyes, studying her as he chewed slowly. "You should eat something."

She smiled, nervously this time. "I will. You mentioned this morning that the oil was yours in name only. What did you mean by that?"

He set down his cutlery and dabbed his mouth with the linen napkin. "You won't talk about yourself, yet I must give."

"Jean, it's an interview. We had a deal."

"I don't see my oil plans as part of the interview, Emma."

"*Everything* in Ubasi is part of you. I don't think you can extract one from the other without missing the picture. Besides, you did mention the oil this morning." She leaned forward in an obvious way that drew attention to her cleavage.

He forced himself to look back up at her face. He was beginning to feel manipulated. Yet this woman was clearly uncomfortable doing whatever she thought she was doing.

"I mentioned it only in relation to your allegation that I had taken the fields for personal gain," he said. "And I'm sorry I did."

"You've discovered enough oil to make you one of the wealthiest men on this planet, Jean."

The leash on his control grew taut. He was too damn edgy to be having this conversation now. He should get up and leave. Yet a part of him couldn't bear the accusation in her voice. Part of him needed her to know he was good, hell alone knew why.

"It'll make Ubasi wealthy, not me," he said coolly. "It's too damn bad it takes something like a massive oil find to bring my country to world attention, *non?*" He leaned forward. "Ubasi was not sexy enough. It was small, poor, war-ravaged. But now?" He watched her steadily. "Now *I* have the country, and now I have something they *all* want." He paused. "Cheap black gold. Now Ubasi is suddenly sexy because we have it. Is that why *you're* interested in me, too, Emma? Because now *I'm* sexy enough for your book sales? Will this interview make you rich, bring you fame?"

Anger sparked in her eyes and her mouth went flat. "Call it sexy if you want, Jean. But we're talking about a lot more than a few barrels here. I'm told there's enough in those oil fields to rival production in Nigeria and Equatorial Guinea combined. And it's all *yours*. At least, since you stole it."

His body began to thrum.

The night suddenly felt unbearably hot. The call of an owl reached them from the sultry jungle outside, and in spite of his anger at her comments, he was turned on by her fire, her challenge. Desire burned through him.

If Laroque stayed with this woman one second longer, he was going to do something he regretted.

He got to his feet, placed his napkin on the table. "This interview is over," he said. He turned to go, but she grabbed his wrist.

He froze, turned slowly back to face her, lust and aggression swirling dangerously like the chemicals of a Molotov cocktail in his gut, just waiting for the spark.

"You're not telling me the whole story, Jean. *Why?*"

"Why should I tell you anything, Emma?"

"Because you don't want to be known as a despot. You don't want to be like your father, that's why."

Her fingers were hot on his skin, feeding the dark sexual energy in him. He stared at her hand as he spoke. "I take only one thing from the oil, Emma." His eyes lifted, lanced hers. "Power. When you have something others want, you are made strong in direct proportion to their need. I have used my new power

to form an alliance with the rebels that govern the
northern jungles of Ubasi, as well as with the under-
ground militias of our neighbors. You see, Emma, all
those rebels want the same thing as I want for
Ubasi—a fair shake."

She removed her hand from his arm. "I don't
understand."

"They see the massive transnationals drawing
oil from *our* delta. They see incredible profits
going to foreign countries. Meanwhile their own
families starve, their land is raped, their rivers are
polluted with oily rainbows that kill their fish and
their game."

"You and the rebels want the West out?"

"No. We just no longer choose to be victims. In
uniting, we have strength. By arming ourselves, we
have negotiating power. We are now forming a pe-
troleum cartel that will, among other things, coordinate oil policy in the Gulf of Guinea, manage supply,
set pricing and stringent environmental rules. *We*—
the people—will control the Gulf, Emma. Anyone
who doesn't like it will have to convince the international community that they have a claim to go to war
over what is ours. And we *will* fight them."

Incredulity filled her eyes. The pulse in her
smooth pale neck pulsed rapidly. "You're *serious.*"

"Do I look like a joker?"

"Jean, you do realize that any one of the superpowers or transnationals *will* fight you for this. They
will go to war to keep the status quo."

He leaned down, close to the gorgeous mouth he just wanted to ravish. "Exactly, Emma. Which is precisely why we are preparing for war." He was so close to kissing her now.

He touched her neck and ran his hand very slowly down to her shoulder, feeling her pulse increase under his fingers. "And you know something else?" he whispered over her lips. "Any one of those superpowers or transnationals you just mentioned are also capable of sending spies into Ubasi to undermine me."

She swallowed nervously.

"But you've seen what happens to those who betray me," he said, his eyes tunneling into hers.

Hot spots appeared on her cheeks. "Do...do the deaths of those four American geologists have anything to do with this plan of yours, Jean?"

"Why should they?"

Her eyes flicked away from his.

"Look at me, Emma."

She lifted her eyes slowly and met his. Her lips were so close he could taste the wine on her breath, he could taste *her.* "You think *I* killed those men because those bodies were displayed in that fashion? After everything I have told you about myself?"

"I...I only—"

He angled her chin, forcing her not to break eye contact. "Do you know something that I don't about those men, Emma?"

Her eyes flickered.

His heart turned cold. He swore viciously, lurched to his full height and stalked out into the hot jungle night.

Laroque knew a liar when he saw one.

Chapter 8

23:03 Zulu. Saturday, November 9.
Ubasi Palace

He didn't trust her.

That much was clear. He was testing her, probably because he didn't yet have any proof she wasn't who she claimed to be. She needed to be more careful. She was walking a very fine line with him.

And she needed to move faster.

Emily's eyes shot to the grandfather clock. In less than an hour she'd have only five days left. If she didn't contact Jacques in that time, they *would* kill him.

Conflict churned inside her. Laroque was a revolutionary, his plan bold, brash. But it *was* conceivable. If he pulled this off it would represent a major power shift in Africa. The corporate interest behind the status quo in Washington wasn't going to allow that—they had way too much vested in African oil right now. Cutting off the supply could send the American economy into an instant downward spiral.

A cold feeling filled her chest. Just how much did Washington actually know?

Were she and the FDS being used as pawns to stop Laroque in this oil game?

It was certainly feasible.

They'd rather see someone like Souleyman in power, someone who could be bought, controlled. Because there was no way in hell anyone could hope to control Jean-Charles Laroque.

A sick feeling leached from her chest to her stomach. This also, however, gave Laroque motive to eliminate the CIA agents, especially if those operatives were informing Washington about his cartel. Emily knew he was capable after seeing what he did today. Yet she honestly did not believe he'd have used his father's signature display of the bodies. It didn't make sense.

Unless she was being manipulated on that front, too.

She was caught in the middle, way over her head. Jacques was probably not aware of the scope of this, either. He would not have accepted this commission otherwise. The FDS walked a fine line in Africa. When in doubt, they erred in the favor of the indigenous populations. Surely Laroque's cartel would be seen as a positive for the people?

She swore softly.

Maybe Jacques did know.

The only thing Emily knew for certain was that absolutely nothing was as it seemed in Ubasi. There were shadows behind shadows, puppeteers behind manipulators.

She wiped her damp palms on her napkin, then pushed back her chair and stood, nerves biting at her stomach. She had to try to learn more from Laroque, because while she'd been sent here to take him down, she might now also be the only person in the world who could save him.

If Jacques did know about this cartel, and she ended up going against him, her career with the FDS would be over. And possibly her life, too.

But without communication she was on her own. She had only Laroque to work with, and she was going to have to go all the way to push him to his limits, to get the information she needed. Because at some point in the next five days she was going to have to pick a side.

It was even hotter out on the wide stone veranda that overlooked the forest. A full moon hung low over the forest canopy, thick and dark with secrets.

The sounds of the night rose from the blackness and drifted on damp and verdant air tinged with the scent of flowers that bloomed only in the dark.

Laroque stood silhouetted against the moonlight, staring out over the jungle—a powerful and lonely specter.

She came up behind him. "Jean?"

He didn't respond.

She reached up and touched his shoulder. He whipped round, moonlight catching his eyes, his pulsing intensity startling her.

Emily took a quick step back.

"I…I'm sorry, Jean. I know you've said you don't condone what your father was, or what he did, but it's impossible to ignore the parallel."

"Don't you see, Emma?" he snarled. "That's exactly what was intended. Someone *wants* the parallel drawn. They want to frame me for those murders."

The hostility in his voice sent shivers over her hot skin.

"Why?" she asked softly.

His eyes narrowed, glinting in the pale light. "I thought I told you this interview was over."

"This is off the record. You need to talk to me, Jean."

"And why would I need to talk to you?"

Because I might be the only one who can save you.

She edged a little closer, and touched his arm tentatively. "Because you have no one else."

His eyes held hers, his energy turning darker, more palpable.

"I have my generals to confide in, Emma. My military advisers, the headmen of the villages, the council I am putting together. Those are the people I look to."

She moved her hand up his arm slightly. Her only chance was to get close to him, to make him care enough so that if she needed to tell him why she was here, he might not hurt her. "I mean just to share, Jean. You can't stand so alone."

"I always have."

"But it hasn't been by choice, has it?"

He said nothing. The moonlight threw an eerie glow off the mica in the cliffs of the distant Purple Mountains.

"What about the hostages, Jean?" she said gently, worried about pushing too far, too fast. "Why did you take those men from Nigeria?"

He swore and cupped her face roughly, his voice lowering to a darkly seductive pitch. "Why won't you give it up, woman?"

She swallowed. She could feel the thrumming strength of his fingers and she could see a muscle pulsing at his jawline. An owl hooted, its shadow momentarily blocking the moon as it swooped over the forest. "Why do you keep answering my questions, then, Jean?" she whispered.

He moved his face closer to hers. "Maybe I need you to understand me." He slid his hand down from her jaw and curled his fingers around her nape, drawing her closer. It was warm and rough against her skin, an outdoorsman's hand. A warrior's hand. A hand capable of love.

And death?

Emily felt herself melt inside, drawn to his complexity, his strange need for her.

He lowered his head, bringing his mouth near hers. "Maybe I want to trust *you*, Emma," he murmured, feathering his lips softly over her mouth.

"Maybe—" he said darkly "—I want to know how *you* know so much about those hostages." He brushed his lips even more firmly over hers, drawing her closer at the same time. "Maybe I want to know how *you* know there are even Americans among them."

Panic unfurled low in her belly. Her breaths became short, making her light-headed. A shriek in the jungle made her jerk back, but he gripped her arm suddenly, rattling her completely.

"I…the science team, the staff at the hotel, they were all talking about it…" Her voice came out in a rough whisper. "About why everyone was being ordered out of the country."

"News travels fast."

She tried to step back again, couldn't. Panic rose in her gut.

He slid his hand down her arm, encircling her wrist. He was edgy, wild.

She didn't feel right, either.

His eyes drilled into hers. "I did *not* kill those men, Emma. And I did not sanction those hostages being taken from Nigeria."

She swallowed, and nodded. "I…I believe you."

"Do you?"

Her eyes began to water. "I do."

His grip relaxed slightly and she exhaled.

"What else do you believe, Emma? Tell me about yourself. Where do *you* come from?"

It was a test. She felt his net closing around her. The flame of panic licked harder at her stomach.

She was a trained operative and a psychologist—she could talk her way out of this. She could control her emotions. But something was wrong. The panic was burning too fast, growing way out of proportion to the situation. Flames flicked through her belly, faster, rising up into her chest, burning through her lungs and searing into her throat.

She couldn't breathe, couldn't speak. She was dizzy. Her pulse began to race.

He was watching her intently, a hunter waiting for his prey to dash so he could strike. A dark breeze suddenly rattled fat leaves. The clapping noise made her jump, unraveling the last little shred of control she held over her mind. Him—this place—it was all getting to her, drilling down into the roots of her psyche where her phobias lay locked away. They were being chiseled free, and were sifting to the surface of her brain, taking hold.

"I…" Her voice choked in her throat. She tried again. "I…think I'm tired. I…need to sleep." She pulled her hand out from his hold and turned to leave, but he caught her arm, spun her back and kissed her hard on the mouth.

She froze momentarily as his mouth pressed over hers, then she melted almost as quickly as heat devoured her from the inside. Her knees buckled, but he caught her, pulling her hard up against his body, his lips moving hungrily and aggressively over hers. Something wild and primal surged violently up from her core, and she met his hunger with a hot urgency of her own, opening her mouth under him, her tongue twisting with his, her teeth scoring his lips, a soft moan releasing from somewhere deep in her chest.

His hand moved up from her waist and cupped her breast roughly. A spasm of pleasure speared right into her belly, and she pressed her pelvis against his thigh, needing to feel him against her.

In the back of her mind she heard the jungle sounds, felt the velvet cloak of humidity over her shoulders, but there was no logic to her thoughts. She moved her hands over his chest, feeling resilient pads of muscle moving under her fingers. It made her hotter, hungrier, and she slid her hands down his belly.

He pulled back abruptly, his breathing ragged, his eyes wild in the silver moonlight. He took her by the shoulders, held her steady, his eyes searching hers for…something, for some answer to an unarticulated question.

Confusion washed through her, and a coolness shivered over the heat of her skin. She suddenly felt embarrassed.

"Emma?" His voice was rough. "Do you want this?"

Her heart was beating so hard she ached. She wanted him like she'd wanted no other man. She wanted to ride his rough energy, tap into his power, obliterate the fears that plagued her mind. One kiss had opened a hunger so raw in her she had no idea it had even existed.

She swallowed.

This was a mistake.

This was a man who could destroy her. This was

her *job*—and he was her subject. Panic separated itself from the heat of her desire and began to writhe inside her again as rational thought resurfaced.

Had she learned nothing in New York?

"I...I can't do this."

She swiftly crossed the veranda and entered the dining hall, the noose of fear tightening, choking her.

She heard him coming behind her.

Her breathing quickened, and she rushed through the palace, right past the guards. She just had to get to her room, get somewhere safe.

"Emma!"

He was coming after her. She could hear his boots. She began to walk faster, faster, her heart pounding as she broke into a run. She knew it made no sense at all, but she couldn't *not* try to escape from the thing she feared the most—the power of her own attraction. The thing she tried to hide from. The fear she pretended she didn't have.

"Emma! Stop!"

He caught up to her, grabbed her arm, spun her round. She was panting, her body drenched in sweat.

"What the hell is going on, Emma? What are you running from?"

You. Everything you represent.

But she said nothing. She looked away, afraid of connecting with his eyes, afraid of his charisma, his growing sensual hold over her.

She should never have touched him. She'd assumed she could handle him.

"Talk to me, Emma," he said softly, feathering her cheek with the backs of his fingers. "It was you who said we needed to talk, remember?"

She struggled to hold back tears. She wanted to lean into his solid chest, feel those hands on her, protective, the way she'd seen they could be. At the same time, it's exactly what she *didn't* want. Off limits professionally or not, this man was bad for her. He had a rotten family record. She had no idea how much of his father lurked inside him.

She'd seen firsthand what men like him could do to women like her. And her mother.

"Who has hurt you, Emma?"

He was astute, she had to hand him that. But she couldn't tell him, not without blowing her cover. She could not tell him about her own father, about her own sick need for powerful men like her dad, and about how that need fed into her fear of being dominated, controlled, like her mother had been.

She couldn't tell him how General Tom Carlin had shaped everything she had become in life—from joining the military to getting her doctorate in psychology, to specializing in the minds of dominant males. She could not tell him how she *still* sought approval from her dad. She couldn't tell Jean about her own mother's suicide.

Emily couldn't even voice it all properly to herself. The only time she'd come close to talking about it was with Anthony. And look where that had got her.

Yet somehow Laroque had unearthed something in her, a yearning to share, to articulate it all.

He'd understand.

He'd seen that same kind of dependency in his mother. It made her feel connected with him because of it, even as the power of her attraction to him frightened her.

She'd been suppressing this all for far too long now, and she craved catharsis.

But Laroque was a stranger. And she was a spy.

She couldn't share.

He took her into his arms, drew her close and gently brushed his lips over her forehead.

It did her in. Tears slid over her cheeks. He kissed them away, and his kisses moved gently, hesitantly closer to her lips, but she placed her hands flat against his chest. "No," she whispered hoarsely. "Not now. I…I'm sorry."

He tilted her chin up gently and brushed a tear from her face with the rough pad of his thumb. "Later, then?"

Emily looked into eyes, softened with compassion, and she knew she was going to sleep with him.

She wanted to.

But she walked away, trying to coordinate limbs that felt like melting jelly.

In the dark hours before dawn, Laroque finally received word that Shaka had pulled through. A savage happiness ripped through his body. He threw back his head, closed his eyes, and he heard the velvet memory of her voice. *You need to share, Jean.* It curled through him. *You can't stand alone.*

He breathed out hard. Emma had opened a door he could no longer shut. She'd let him taste a need.

Laroque left his dog sleeping peacefully in his basket, and he took the stairs up to her room.

He knocked gently, listened, but there was no answer. He hesitated. He shouldn't do this. Then he thought of the sultry promise he'd seen in her violet eyes when he'd said "later." It was a look of longing that went well beyond the invitation he'd tasted on her lips.

He reached for the handle, opened her door, slowly.

She lay in a silver puddle of moonshine, louvered doors wide open to the hot sultry night, her sheets in a wild tangle on the floor. She wore only a thin white camisole and panties.

His pulse fluttered.

Her arm was hooked behind her head, displaying breasts that were small and firm under the sheer white fabric. Her skin was the color of alabaster in the moonlight and it was sheened with heat, giving her an ethereal quality. Her hair fanned out darkly over the white pillow. She was breathing deeply, fast asleep. He ran his eyes down her body, his mouth going dry.

The knee of her right leg was crooked, the ankle hooked loosely under her other knee in a way that opened to hint at the dark delta between her thighs.

His stomach swooped sharply and his breath

lodged tight in his throat. He gripped the door handle. He should leave. Now. Quickly. He should never have come in like this.

But he couldn't. Not after seeing her like this.

His heart began to bang hard against his chest wall, the rhythm echoing in a hot, heavy pulse between his legs.

"Emma?" he whispered, his voice rough.

Her lashes fluttered and she moaned softly, lifting and repositioning her hips in such a way that spat fire to his groin.

"Emma?"

She moved again, opening her eyes, staring straight at him.

"Jean?" she murmured.

He stepped into her room and shut the door quietly behind him.

Chapter 9

Emily had fallen asleep angry.

She'd returned to her quarters furious at losing control. She'd allowed her personal issues to interfere with a job in a way that was absolutely inexcusable, and she'd totally embarrassed herself.

She was going to take a break after this job. She needed to totally reassess her life, her career. That business with Anthony had been a wake-up call. She should have faced it, dealt with it properly before taking on another FDS contract. But, damn, she hadn't wanted to, even though the therapist in her knew it would have been the right path.

Shrinks were notoriously inept at dealing with their own neuroses. It's why they went into the profession in the first place—they were all bloody nuts.

It was with these irritable thoughts that Emily fell into a hot and tangled sleep. And once again, Le Diable emerged from black shadows and entered her dream. Once again the night was hot and velvet, and he was touching her in ways she shouldn't imagine.

"Emma?" The voice in her dream sent a low shiver of cool along the damp heat of her skin.

"Emma." She heard it again, his rolling bass turning thick, tugging at something elemental in her gut. She moaned softly, lifting her hips, feeling the ache in her belly for him again. She was hot, so hot.

She sensed him materializing from the darkness, coming closer, and the ache began to throb sharp and low in her pelvis. She instinctively opened her thighs a little wider as she moaned again, trying to escape the heat, trapped somewhere deep and humid in her dream. She felt a slight breeze ripple over her skin—a sense of real presence.

He was standing there. At her door.

She stared straight at him, her mind confused, her body still hot, ready. "Jean?"

He came to the bed, sat down beside her, the moonlight glinting in his pale eyes. "You are so beautiful, Emma," he said, gently tracing the line of her jaw with his fingers. Her nipples contracted sharply under her skimpy camisole as he watched. "I need you, Emma. But…just say the word," he whispered, "and I'll leave."

She shook her head, and he continued tracing his fingers down along the contour of her breast, circling around her hard nipple. Her eyelids fluttered and molten heat settled low in her belly.

He leaned over her. "Are you sure?"

She moistened her lips. Not trusting herself to speak, she reached for the hem of her camisole and pulled it over her head, then drew him down to her. He covered her mouth firmly with his, lowering his weight onto her.

He was hot, his body solid muscle, his military fatigues rough against her bare breasts. He moved his lips gently over hers in hesitant question, making any decision to move further solely hers.

She tried to think, but she couldn't. Didn't even want to. She wanted Jean, and she was ready for him. And she didn't give a damn about anything else in this world right at this moment. She needed this fundamental human connection.

She needed to feel like a wanted woman.

She just needed *him*.

She kissed him back, hard. Hungry. Desperate. Opening his mouth wider with her lips, she tangled her tongue slickly with his as she yanked his shirt out of his pants and rapidly worked the buttons. She splayed open his shirt and moaned involuntarily against his mouth as her hands met the firm skin of his iron-solid abs.

He lifted her buttocks, removing her panties, positioning her in the center of the king-size bed as he kissed her. Then he sat back and removed his clothes, his eyes never leaving hers until he stood fully naked.

He studied her brazenly, raking his eyes down the length of her hot, damp body in such a way she could feel them moving on her skin, stopping to rest on the mound between her thighs. A dark smile of satisfaction curled over his mouth and he leaned forward, placed his hands on her knees, opened her wider. He bent down and she felt the slick, hot tip of his tongue at the apex of her thighs. Emily bit back the sound that swelled from her chest. She closed her eyes, threw her head back, unable to control the shiver of her muscles as he flicked his tongue between her legs, going a little deeper each time, swirling, teasing. But when his teeth grazed the exquisitely sensitive little nub at her centre, the sound escaped her control, and she began to shake.

He lifted her hips higher, drawing her to himself, entering her with his tongue, going deeper with a wild and increasing hunger of his own until she felt she was going to explode.

But just as she was convinced she could hold back her climax no longer, he stopped abruptly.

Emily lay there, shaking, trying to catch her breath, the air suddenly cool between her legs.

He moved up, his body covering hers, heavy. She felt his knees pushing hers apart even farther, giving better access, and with one sharp and powerful thrust he entered her fully. She gasped, opening herself wider, arching her back, wanting him even deeper. He filled her completely, hot, hard and thick.

And he moved inside her, fast, quick strokes that seared her nerves. Limbs intertwined in a breathless, elemental rhythm that cut through the intellectual tangle of games and lies straight to the raw, physical core where the bond was rudimentary, savage and simple.

He rolled her on top of him so that she straddled him, knees wide on either side of his body. She sat back, sinking deeper onto his erection. She braced her hands on his shoulders, hair falling wild over her face, and she rocked her hips, breasts bouncing as he bucked under her, forcing himself deeper into her, so deep that she suddenly exploded with a rough cry. She'd never needed a man so badly, been so ready for him, that she'd screamed with the raw pleasure of release.

She was panting as he spun her over and sank back into her. He held her tight as he drove repeatedly into her before finding his own release with a powerful shudder that took control of his body.

They lay like that, in the puddle of silver moonlight, hot and intertwined, still breathing hard, neither of them wishing to break contact with each other or shatter the moment with speech.

Emily felt Jean's pulse gradually begin to slow and his body relax against hers, and a deep sense of physical peace washed through her.

She watched the shadows on the whitewashed walls, feeling at a loss to describe the sensation of just lying here, holding this powerful man naked against her skin as he fell asleep in her bed. So she didn't try. She just savored his body with a rare sense of belonging just in the moment.

They'd both known that he'd come to her tonight, that this would happen. They also both knew that something had shifted.

For whatever reasons they'd been compelled to this point. Where they would go from now, Emily had no idea.

06:33 Zulu. Sunday, November 10.
Ubasi Palace

Laroque propped himself up onto his elbow and moved a strand of dark hair from Emma's face. This morning she was a different person. She was a woman strong in her own sexuality, one who could give as hard as she got. Yet he'd glimpsed her vulnerability inside. This dichotomy intrigued him. He understood it. He knew himself how to be potently powerful while balancing on the shaky foundations of a rough childhood.

He knew how to bottle fear behind a cool facade of control, because giving your enemy the scent of weakness gave him an edge. It could cost the battle, and your life.

He wondered—not for the first time—if he needed to protect himself from Emma.

He trailed his finger slowly down her belly, smiling as she shivered slightly and opened sleepy eyes. He could make love to her forever—but he still knew virtually nothing about her.

"Do you want to talk about what happened after dinner?"

She closed her eyes and shook her head.

He didn't press it. He didn't want to break the connection they had right now.

Perhaps he just didn't want to acknowledge that the reason she was unable to talk about herself was because she was hiding the truth about who she really was, and why she was in his palace.

He lay back, choosing instead to be content in the moment as a pale dawn leaked into the sky. But his beeper sounded, slicing reality back into the morning.

Laroque tensed. Groping around the floor, he found his pants, took his pager from his pocket and read the message. He dressed quickly as she watched him, a growing wariness in her eyes.

He kissed her softly. "I have to go. I'll be back before dark."

She sat up, eyes strangely purple in the dim light. "Where are you going?"

He paused. "There's been an incursion. A skirmish with Souleyman's men near one of the villages. Several of his militants are dead. I need to take a look. My people need to talk to me."

She opened her mouth to speak and he covered her lips with his fingers. "Don't worry. I'll be back before dinner."

And he was gone.

Emily flopped back onto the bed.

What had she just done to the mission, to herself?

She got up, hair falling in a damp tangle over her shoulders, and padded barefoot onto the small stone balcony. The dawn sun was warm on her naked body. And for a moment, she didn't want the tangle of complications of her life. She didn't want to think about the FDS backing Souleyman, or the cloak-and-dagger operations of this mission. She just wanted to feel like an Eve, in the soft morning sun blanketing this Eden.

She closed her eyes, relishing the sensation on her skin, and with mild shock she realized that for the first time in a long, long while, she actually felt physically whole.

It was a sensation she didn't want to lose. It was a state she hadn't even known she'd been searching for. And she'd finally found it—in the wrong place, with the wrong man. She was falling for the enemy.

But *was* he?

She opened her eyes and stared out over the forest canopy. The jungle looked even more beautiful today. That made it deceptive, and even more threatening, because this jungle was not an easy place to survive. It was one of the most competitive arenas on earth, a place where you either hunted or *were* hunted, killed or *were* killed.

And she wasn't sure whether she was pawn, or power.

Somewhere out there, the *real* enemy might lie.

All Emily knew for certain this morning was that regardless of what Jean was doing, it was not in her to condemn him to death.

But that's exactly what would happen if she didn't find a way to break her radio silence—he would die.

In less than five days.

Laroque's Jeep pulled into a village which lay at the religious heart of his country. The headman of this community was a key ally of his, and a friend. Descended from noble warrior tradition, he was not only an astute military strategist, he was a persuasive orator, too. He also had a keen grasp of what was of traditional importance to Ubasi. This was a man Laroque hoped would form part of a powerful Ubasi democracy in a few years. He wanted him in cabinet.

He swung out of the Jeep and strode through the circle of mud dwellings toward the headman's hut. Laroque visited here often, but this was the first time he'd walked without Shaka at his side. He'd checked on his dog before leaving the palace, and things were looking good. Shaka had turned a corner. He was definitely going to make it. But the shock of nearly losing something so close to him had shifted Laroque's world slightly.

Making love to Emma had further unsettled him. He was falling for her, and that was going to make things difficult, especially if he learned she was deceiving him.

This alone put a kind of fierceness into Laroque's stride—he *wanted* her to be who she claimed she was. He wanted it so badly he was worried it would skew his judgment.

He instinctively felt for his weapon before ducking into the hut. He'd been called to this village because of an emergency during the night. The headman's soldiers had engaged in a shoot-out with a group of what appeared to be Souleyman insurgents. As far as Laroque knew, the so-called insurgents had all been killed. It was their bodies he'd been called to see, and he was keen to check their uniforms, weapons and communications equipment. He welcomed any small clue that might help him ascertain what the hell he was up against.

But as Laroque moved the bead curtain aside with the back of his hand, he saw it was not the headman, but the village *feticheuse* sitting in the center of the hut. The old fortune-teller squatted in the dull yellow glow of a paraffin lamp, as if waiting for him.

Laroque froze, almost backed out, until he saw the headman sitting on a small wooden stool across the room. He raised his arm, motioned for Laroque to enter. "I'm having my shells read, come in."

The wizened old woman stared at Laroque with cloudy eyes as she drew a handful of cowrie shells and worn ivory pieces from a leather bag. She cast them across her mat with a rattle.

She began to sway in rhythm to a moaning chant that sent a shiver over Laroque's skin. He had a sense it was not the headman's fortune being read, but his own. "I'll wait outside," he said.

But as he moved, the woman stopped dead. Her eyes flared, pupils rolling back, leaving glassy whites. "Yah!" she whispered, and refocused on Laroque. His heart lurched. The woman's one word had punched him physically in the stomach. He backed out quickly and stepped into the hot sun. A sheen of perspiration had formed over his forehead. He swiped it off with the back of his arm. Damn, this stuff could get to one.

"What the hell was that about?" he asked the headman as he finally emerged from the hut.

He studied Laroque intently. "Come," he said. "I must show you the bodies."

The headman led Laroque along a narrow jungle path to where the slain militants had been left in dense undergrowth. The forest was very dark, little light filtering through the dense canopy.

Flies and insects buzzed over the victims, settling on wounds.

Laroque tried to ignore the smell as he crouched down to examine them. "They're not locals," he said, moving one man onto his back.

The headman nodded. "Looks like hired guns from the Sahara region. Word is that's where Souleyman is getting his muscle. Those guys don't come cheap."

Laroque pursed his lips as he checked pockets. The uniforms were devoid of any insignia. He found no ID at all. "What about weapons?" he asked as he stood up.

"Czech-made Rachot UK-68s. Right out the box."

Laroque whistled. These guys had been carrying highly portable general-purpose machine guns, not the sort of weapons commonly found floating around African war zones.

"Where are the guns?"

"Back at the village."

Laroque frowned. "You find any communications equipment on them?"

The headman nodded. "It's also back at the village."

Laroque narrowed his eyes. "Why'd you bring me out here, then?"

The headman glanced nervously over his shoulder, then stepped closer.

A foreboding rustled through Laroque, raising the hairs on the back of his neck. He automatically felt for his weapon, every sense suddenly on keen alert, even as he maintained an outward cool.

"It's not the bodies I wanted you to see," the headman said, his voice low, his eyes intense, his face dark in the jungle shadow. "It's what that man—" he pointed to one of the bloodied bodies with the business end of his Kalashnikov "—told us before we killed him."

A muscle tightened over Laroque's chest. "What did he say?"

"He said that Le Diable is bewitched, that a sorceress has come to destroy him, and she is stealing his power."

"What!"

"He said that this witch is living in Le Diable's

castle, that she has hair like a raven and eyes like the Purple Mountains." He paused, the intensity of his eyes darkening to a smoldering black. "Do you remember the prophecy, Jean?"

"*What* prophecy?" But even as Laroque asked the question, he registered the earlier origins of his unease with Emma, the whispers of warning he'd felt when looking into her violet eyes, that feeling he'd forgotten something.

"When you came and took power from Souley-man," the headman said, "the Ubasi high priestess ordained you would hold power until a woman arrived and changed everything. Do you recall that the priestess said this woman would have eyes like the Purple Mountains?"

Laroque swore and dragged his hand over his hair. "This is ridiculous! I didn't believe it then, and I don't now."

But something *had* stuck in his mind—some dark little seed that had given rise to the sense of warning that something about Emma was dangerous, something that went beyond the obvious.

He cursed to himself. He'd been too damn busy overtaking the country and installing some kind of functional government to worry about the mumblings of some ambitious high priestess. It had been a mistake. Voodoo magic was the spiritual backbone of this country. He'd used it himself to gain power.

He glanced around. The forest was impenetrable here. It felt ominous, as if it had eyes. He cursed again. It was *him,* his mind, already playing tricks on him. It was that damned fortune teller.

He was giving it all value, emotion, where none existed. But *this* was where a curse, a prophecy, played with your head. You had to get it out of your mind, because it could drive you mad, make you paranoid, like it had Souleyman.

"So what?" Laroque snapped. "So what if they say this? It means nothing!"

The headman looked hard at him, and Laroque realized he'd have to tread carefully. He'd been done a favor in this man's eyes. This was a tribal leader who dealt with superstition on a daily basis.

"It means nothing to *me,*" he added.

"It means something to your people, Jean," the man answered. "To your people this holds real power. Souleyman knows of the prophecy, and through his spies he has learned of the woman in your presence. He is using this—coincidence or not—to spread the word that you are growing weak, that it is time for change to once again come for Ubasi. Souleyman has made this prophecy something you need to reckon with."

So Souleyman was using the religion just as he had—as a military and propaganda tool. The headman was right—you ignored this stuff at your peril. You had to fight it at the same level. Denying it, laughing at the priestess, would mean mocking his people's religion—mocking *them.*

"The rumors that Souleyman spreads, they travel

fast, Jean. You must stop them, and this is why I brought you here, to talk to you away from the eyes and ears of people who are searching you for weakness. Before it is too late. The Ubasi people can not be allowed to think you are weakening, Jean."

"I'm not, dammit! You know that." Although suddenly he wasn't so sure. After his night with Emma, he *felt* different.

A bird shrieked up high in the canopy.

Laroque jerked at the sound, then angrily spun on his heels and marched out of the grove, leaving the bodies behind. The headman followed as Laroque moved swiftly along the narrow jungle path, hacking unnecessarily at undergrowth with his machete, beating back things that stood in his way. He would *not* let anything stop him. He refused to allow some woman to steal his dream.

He stepped out into harsh sunlight where a group of his soldiers waited, but the colors looked different. Laroque imagined he could see a new wariness in the eyes of his men.

He was getting paranoid. He couldn't have that.

"The woman—" the headman whispered over his shoulder "—she must go."

Jean nodded curtly, saluted his men and got back into his Jeep. Without his dog.

Did they notice that, too? That his "spirit dog" was missing?

For the first time since he'd sailed into Ubasi, Laroque felt slightly unsure of himself. The headman was right. Emma had to go. There was too much at stake right now, and perception was everything.

But first he needed to know where her laptop was broadcasting to. He could send her out of the country without her computer. However, if Mano Ndinga *did* find something highly incriminating on her machine, Laroque needed her to answer questions.

He might even need her for leverage.

For that he had to keep her, at least until Mano arrived.

Never mind the other more personal reasons he felt like keeping her around. He'd been a fool. He'd been seduced by a woman he suspected could be an operative. He'd thought he could handle it. He had not anticipated the reach of her power over him.

Irritated, he snapped open his phone as he ordered his driver to move. "Any sign of Mano?" he barked into his cell over the growl of the engine.

"Yes. Ndinga's come early—just arrived."

Laroque closed his eyes briefly. "Give him the computer!"

He snapped his phone closed. Within hours he'd have an answer, then he'd have to deal with Emma. In a way that satisfied his people.

Chapter 10

It was early evening when Laroque returned to the castle compound. They told him Emma was down at the pool. He instructed his men not to bother them for a while, to close off that section of the garden.

He marched over the lawn, adrenaline thumping through his veins. He should have gone straight to see Mano, but he wanted to see her first, before he was told she was some kind of spy, that she was here to destroy him. The evening was incredibly hot, the air fecund. Distant evening drums reverberated over the forest. The cry of a fish eagle split the air, and small fruit bats flitted almost imperceptibly over a sky deepening to violet and purple. Like her eyes.

Like the eyes in that damn prophecy.

She *was* a curse. She'd stolen his focus.

He'd allowed it to happen to himself.

Such was the power of this strange religion.

He should never have slept with her, allowed himself to feel anything. Because he *did*—something that went well beyond whatever little charade they were playing.

But he had to put an end to it now—

He stopped dead.

Swallowed.

She was coming out of water that shimmered in dark, inky ripples behind her. Her underwear was doubling as a bathing suit. Wet, it left nothing—absolutely nothing—to the imagination.

A black slip of lace nestled between her thighs, and two small triangles outlined her breasts. In contrast, her skin was white, luminous. She shook her hair and a spray of droplets fell like black pearls to the dark water.

His arousal was instantaneous. Explosive. Hot.

He didn't allow himself to think. He began to walk. Steadily. Right up to her.

She stilled as he neared, her eyes reflecting the colors in the sky, water glistening over her skin. He fixated on a smooth rivulet that slithered from the base of her breasts down to her belly button, where it pooled momentarily before reaching a tipping point and sliding farther to disappear into the dark fabric at the apex of her thighs.

He looked up and met her eyes. The connection

was visceral, electric. Her breathing quickened, and her lips parted slightly.

In the back of his mind he could hear the beat of the drums, the sounds of evening in the forest canopy. The thick scent of flowers in his garden was sweet and provocative.

He lifted her hair away from her breasts, and through the sheer fabric of her bra he could see her nipples were hard. His groin ached as another shaft of hot need cut through him.

He cupped her breast roughly. She caught her breath, but she didn't step back.

Instead she tilted her chin and locked eyes with him. He met the dare in her gaze as he grazed her nipple, catching the nub between his thumb and fore-finger. She swallowed and squared her shoulders slightly, which only lifted her nipples a little higher and shifted them in his direction.

He began to pound with need, barely able to breathe.

He reached for the clasp between her breasts, undid her bra, slid the straps over her shoulders and dropped the wet fabric to the shallow water in which she still stood. A sultry heat darkened her eyes. She wanted him. Right here.

Well, he wanted her.

With one hand he yanked his shirt over his head, and with the other he pushed her back into the water, deeper and deeper, waves sloshing and slapping gently between her legs as she moved.

He followed her in, pushing her in front of him,

water soaking into his pants. He guided her back toward the small waterfall that tumbled into his rock pool, undoing his fly as he moved, his eyes never leaving hers. The splash of water around them drove him higher. He grabbed her thigh, lifted her leg around him, yanked the scrap of lace aside and entered her sharply, pushing in deep.

She gasped, lifted her leg higher, broadening access for him as her nails dug into his back. She arched into him, moving with him, meeting his hunger with a voracious need of her own.

He lifted her other leg, wrapped it firmly around himself and held her hips as he thrust. She threw her head back, digging her fingers into his hair, finding purchase, gripping tightly as he moved faster, urged on by the searing pain of his desire. The water was syrupy and warm as it slicked between them, and she came so fast and suddenly it shocked him. A cry escaped her throat, drowned by the sound of the water, as she threw her head far back, her breasts exposed, her muscles clamping down on him, until she went limp.

He was still hard as rock. He lowered her, spun her around, braced her palms up against the rock. And he reentered her from behind, taking her in a way as elemental as the jungle around them.

They sat in silence beside the pool as it grew dark. Words defied what was happening between them, and the cloak of night felt comfortable. Laroque had wrapped the towel she'd brought down to the pool around his waist and given her his T-shirt. She looked almost girlish with her wet hair slicked back—so clean and innocent and pure. Yet there was nothing innocent about the way he'd taken her in the pool, nor in her desire for him. She was a mystery to Laroque, mostly because he couldn't fathom the source of their undeniable bond, given the circumstances. In spite of it all, he was still falling for this woman. Did she feel the same about him? Or was this an act?

He couldn't put it off. Not a moment longer. He had to go and see Mano in the communications room. He needed to put an end to this insecurity. He needed to know who she was.

He touched the side of her face gently. A part of him wanted to hold on to her for just one moment longer before it all blew apart. He had no idea what he'd do with her if he found evidence she'd come to destroy him. She could have hurt him, killed him, several times over if that's what she'd been trained and sent to do. He took some solace in the fact that she hadn't. It gave him hope.

She seemed distracted. "Hey there, *mon petite,* where've you gone?"

Her eyes whipped to his, suddenly vulnerable, then her subtle mask was back. His heart sank just a little.

She smiled, but it never quite reached those mystical eyes. "I was just thinking about tomorrow."

"What about it?"

She shrugged, and looked sad.

His pager bleeped. Twice. Thank God the thing still worked, thought Laroque as he fished it from his wet pocket.

He checked the messages—there were two.

Mano needed him ASAP, and the hostages had finally arrived at the rebel base camp.

"I have something I must attend to," he said.

"I'll stay out here a bit."

He hesitated. "It's getting dark."

"I'll be fine—you have guards everywhere, Jean." She smiled wistfully, her eyes hauntingly luminous in the dusky light. " I…I just need a while. To think."

He frowned, nodded and strode up the garden toward his palace, a knot tightening in his gut.

Emily drew her knees up close to her chest and hugged them tight. Anxiety ate at her. She was sinking deeper, falling more and more for this enigmatic man, the line between professional and personal blurring, making it difficult to be objective. She wasn't sure whether she could believe everything he claimed to be doing, but she *wanted* to. She sensed something truly noble inside Jean. In his sister's village she'd witnessed firsthand where his priorities lay. His people not only loved him, they *respected* him. So did his staff. He was tough, but that's what it often took to be a leader, especially in an environment like this. And underneath it all, she could see that he was just human—a man who needed family and a place to belong. A man who needed to protect the things—and people—he cared for. A man who made *her* feel like a complete woman.

Whatever his bold plans for this entire region, whatever his unorthodox methods, Jean-Charles Laroque had more integrity than most of the powerful men Emily had met in Manhattan. And he could do things to her body that no man ever had.

She closed her eyes, stress warring with a sense of duty to her mission and the growing tenderness ballooning inside her chest. By dawn she had four days left.

She had to pick a side.

Her mission. Or this man.

She couldn't have both.

"There is no way in hell this is an ordinary civilian system, Jean."

Tension streamed through Laroque. "Mathieu suspected as much," he said. "It's why I wanted you to take a deeper look at it."

Mano touched his fingertips to her equipment. "This laptop has been equipped with a rocket homing device."

His heart slammed once, then it thumped, steady, fast, hard. His throat tightened and his mouth went bone dry. "*What* did you say?"

"I took it apart, found a missile homing device in the hard drive."

Laroque stared at her computer, thinking about what he and Emma had just done in the pool. Bitterness filled his throat at the thought she had purposefully set out to seduce him, that she felt nothing. "Speak, Mano, tell me more."

"This machine—" he tapped the computer lightly "—is telling someone *right now* exactly what room in your palace it's in. The homing device can either be activated manually from this system, which could then be strategically placed close to a desired target, or it can be activated remotely from the same place to which it is now sending a satellite signal. Someone out on a ship, for example, could launch a warhead and hit whomever is holding this computer within minutes."

Fury burned in Laroque. He walked slowly to the dog basket he'd had brought into the room. He crouched down and touched Shaka's shaved fur softly, watched as his dog's gentle eyes turned trustingly to him.

His eyes shot back to Mano, but his voice remained absolutely level. "Why could Mathieu not see this immediately?"

"He saw there was *something* going on, Jean, and he told you what he could. But until we could take this thing apart in a forensic lab environment free of dust and static, there was nothing definitive. Even so, you need to know how to look for something like this. Look—" He pulled up a screen on a separate monitor.

"I took photos of her hard drive, enlarged them. See here?" He pointed. "This is where the homing apparatus is located. The device is barely visible to the naked eye. It contains sophisticated nanotechnology, is extremely small and deadly effective." He looked up. "You can't get this stuff on the open market, Jean. This is cutting-edge military technology."

"So you put the system back together leaving the homing device intact? It can still be activated?"

Mano's mouth twisted into a wry angle. "That's why I needed to see you ASAP. I don't have the skill to disable something like this without sending an alert directly to whoever is monitoring this thing. And I don't want to risk destroying it totally. It could be booby-trapped to trigger a missile launch instantly. A target-seeking warhead could launch the second I destroy this device, following the pulse of the last recorded coordinates like an echo." He held Laroque's eyes. "The rocket would still hit its target."

"Can you tell where it was manufactured?"

"No. There are no markings, no serial numbers, nothing. I've read about this technology, but I haven't actually seen anything quite like it yet. It could be anything, from Russian-, Chinese-, British- to U.S.-manufactured."

Laroque stroked his dog gently, as red-hot rage boiled inside him.

There was no doubt now. Absolutely none.

He almost shook under the strain of maintaining outward muscular control as he wrapped his mind around the sense of betrayal. Still, he could not stop himself from asking, "Is there no way that perhaps a science crew might have something like this—"

Mano shot his boss a sharp, querulous look. "No, Jean. No way."

Laroque sucked air very deep into his lungs. He stood up from Shaka's basket slowly, battling to subdue the fire of his rage, his feral impulse to storm out and physically confront Emma Sanford. He didn't like the violent urge pumping through his veins.

Had his father felt like this before rage had blinded and erupted from him, before he'd started hurting women? How had Peter Laroque lost control the very first time? And how much more quickly had the violence flared the second and third times? Was it the sense of betrayal of love, even if imaginary, that had driven his dad there the first time?

Distress twisted into Laroque's rage. It hurt. He hadn't felt this deeply rejected since he was a young boy. It made him furious with her, and with himself for being led by his libido.

Even more serious was the fact his staff would now see this proof of her betrayal as concrete evidence of the prophecy. This woman was challenging him in ways he'd never experienced.

She'd stolen his control. And she was threatening his country.

But he would not succumb to brute force. To do so would be his ultimate defeat.

If he wanted to get to the people controlling her, he had to stay very cool and continue to play her game. And he needed a strategy.

"If we move the computer to an outside location," he said calmly, "could we destroy the device with minimal collateral damage?"

"We could. But they will see it being moved. How that might play out is anyone's guess."

"So the GPS is showing them wherever that thing goes?" Laroque said, thinking aloud as he paced the room.

"Correct."

He stilled, bit the inside of his lip. "And you can't tell me *exactly* where it's transmitting to?"

Mano pulled up another screen. "Somewhere here, in this region along the west coast of Africa." He pointed with his pen. "The monitoring station could be on land or sea, but I can't tell you anything more precise. Not yet."

"When?"

"Her system is configured to send a low-strength satellite signal while at rest, and this signal is being rerouted through several hubs to throw electronic tracks. At this level of emission, I can't trace it. However, if her laptop is fired up, and an encrypted code entered, it'll ramp up to full signal strength. Whatever she then types into the computer is transmitted directly to a monitor off-site."

"So you're telling me that this laptop is essentially her communications system? Whatever she enters is relayed live to a screen somewhere else?"

· Mano nodded. "With the signal at full strength for a few seconds, I could triangulate and pinpoint the exact location."

"So with her computer in a resting phase like this, whoever is watching her has no way of knowing whether it's actually in her possession or not? All they know is that it's in my castle?"

"To the best of my knowledge."

"Presumably, then, they'd refrain from activating the missile device unless there was some kind of distress signal from her, because they'd hurt *her* in the attack?"

"That would be my assumption, but—it's a risky one, Jean. This puppy is as good as a live bomb."

Laroque rubbed his face with both hands. "Is it possible to set it up so that if she enters her code, ramps up the signal and begins to communicate on that thing we can pick up her transmission on a monitor down here in the communications room?"

Mano pursed his lips and hummed in a low tone as he toyed with the logistics. "It'll take some time to configure things in such a way that doesn't clue either her or the other party into the fact we're watching them, but I think I can do it."

"And then you'd be able to pinpoint the precise location of the off-site monitor."

"Yes."

"Do it!"

Laroque leaned over a desk and pressed an intercom button, summoning his general.

The man arrived promptly, clicked his heels and stood at attention.

When Laroque spoke, his voice was ruthlessly cool. "Evacuate the palace of civilian staff. Retain only key military personnel. Do it as quietly and calmly as possible."

"Anything else, sir?"

"No. Thank you."

His general hesitated. "What about the woman, sir?"

"She stays. She must know nothing." Laroque turned back to Mano and pointed to her computer. "I am the target of that thing," he said. "I'm banking on the fact her people don't want to hurt her, and unless she sends a distress signal, they won't activate that device. I'll be safe, as long as I keep her close. For my own protection, for Ubasi's protection, she must not for one minute think she is in any real danger."

"It's a gamble, Jean."

He tensed his jaw. Mano didn't know the half of it. "I know. But I must find out who this woman is working for. If we learn *who,* we will know why. From there we can take action. Set her up, Mano. Have me paged when you're ready to roll." He hesitated. "The *instant* you are ready, *comprends?*"

"*Oui.*"

Laroque turned sharply to his other aide. "I need you to do something for me. I want you to take the doctor and Shaka and whatever equipment the doctor may need to my sister's village. Tell the doctor he will be handsomely compensated. Tell him…" Emotion banked sharply in his throat. "Tell him to take care of Shaka."

He whirled on his heels and stormed out, boots echoing loudly down the cold and empty stone corridors.

* * *

She glanced up as he entered the dining room.

Laroque stood stone still at what he saw, his mind shattering into a kaleidoscope of emotions.

She was wearing the turquoise fabric the women in Tamasha's village had given her, nothing else underneath. Her hair had been piled up on her head, exposing the long, pale column of her neck.

He couldn't breathe.

She was so beautiful. So lethal.

His enemy, wrapped in the traditional cloth of his village. His people. His country. And she was here to destroy them all.

Fury hummed through his body.

Laroque had looked his enemy right in the eyes before killing him more times than he could count. But his foe had never been a woman.

This time when he looked into the eyes of his bewitching adversary, a whisper of doubt unsettled the steel of his will.

Whoever had sent this woman had known just how to get under his guard, and into his fortress. Right into his damn bed.

"Jean?"

He inhaled sharply, bracing against the allure of her voice, her body in that cloth. She was going to be his hostage, and she wasn't even going to know it.

"I can't dine with you tonight, Emma," he said simply. "I have meetings. Be ready to leave at first light, we're going north. We'll be gone at least two, maybe three days."

A wariness crept into her eyes. "Why?"

"The hostages have arrived at base camp. I'm going to question them."

Her eyes narrowed, grew calculating. Why had he not noticed that look before?

"Why do you want to take *me?*"

"Because you won't be safe here alone."

And that was a fact. If his men believed she was a sorceress out to destroy him, they were loyal enough to Laroque to eliminate her on his behalf, if he didn't do it himself.

He knew the ways of the jungle well enough, and he needed her alive, as his prisoner.

But although he had to keep his enemy close, the longer she was with him, the more his men were going to question his power to rule. He would lose their faith if they believed the ridiculous notion that he was under her spell, and doing nothing to stop it. He was in a double bind.

"I think I'd prefer to stay in the castle, Jean," she said firmly. "I'd like to spend some time writing up my notes."

"I'm sure you would."

He was also damn sure she'd go looking for her laptop in his absence. She'd try to find a way to communicate. There was not a shred of doubt in Laroque's mind she was an operative, and any spy worth her lies would not underestimate a man of his reputation. She'd know he had to have her computer in his possession, and she'd go looking for it at the first possible chance.

He wasn't going to give her that chance.

And if he was her, he'd also be nervous that something incriminating may already have been discovered in the laptop.

This woman was playing a very dangerous game, but if he'd underestimated her, she'd seriously misjudged him.

"We had a deal," he said flatly. "You're coming with me."

Chapter 11

20:07 Zulu. Sunday, November 10.
FDS base camp. São Diogo Island

Jacques and his crew watched the bank of LCD screens.

April Ngomo, one of Jacques's FDS techs, had summoned them to the situation room, alerting them to a small hiccup in Emily Carlin's computer signal. It had made April uncomfortable.

"It's back on track now," she told them in her rich, melodious voice. "The homing device is still intact, but something definitely interfered with her GPS signal."

"You think someone opened up her system?"

"It's possible."

The tension in the room mounted as they watched the steadily pulsing dot of luminous green on the monitor. "We still have a fix on the GPS in her laptop, right?" Jacques said, nodding toward the dot. "She's in that castle."

"Her computer is," April corrected. "That's all we can say for certain. She should have filed a report by now, Jacques."

"She's not using the laptop because she's not with it." The blunt statement came from Dr. Hunter McBride, FDS surgeon. Jacques had asked him to step into the communications room. Before requalifying as a surgeon, Hunter had been Jacques's top Africa guerrilla warfare expert, and his advice in strategy sessions remained invaluable.

"Either that," said Jacques, "or she's being too closely watched. She did say she'd be out of communication for a while."

"Perhaps she said it under duress," said Hunter.

"No, she'd have sent a coded message. We'll give her the full seven days. That's her brief. She'll do her best to meet it." He glanced at the computerized clock. "If Carlin doesn't make contact by the deadline, we move. We get her out, we activate the homing device."

"I don't like it," said Hunter watching the dot. "If Le Diable finds out she's working for us, she's dead. It's that simple." He looked at Jacques. "She may be already."

"No one ever said this was a safe business. She knew that going in."

Hunter nodded, his eyes serious. He jammed his hands into his fatigue pockets and jerked his chin toward the monitors. "How's the rest of our team placed?"

"The guys are beginning to mobilize with Souleyman's militia here in the east," said April, pointing her pen at a cluster of small flicking red triangles on the map. "The others are in position in the south, over there. We have the choppers on standby in Cameroon."

"Good. Contact me if anything changes, April." Jacques motioned with his head that he needed to talk to Hunter outside. They walked into the night together.

"I ran the IDs on those hostages," he told Hunter.

"You didn't like what you found?"

"They're mercs."

Hunter whistled through his teeth. "Working for who?"

"I don't know. Nothing's adding up. Two of the hostages are Nigerian and three are U.S. citizens by birth. I haven't got much on the Nigerians yet, but neither of those three Americans has been back to the homeland for decades. One is ex-military, was court-martialed, and discharged in connection with prisoner abuse. He left the U.S. shortly afterward. The other two have rough reputations with foreign private security companies and have hired out to wildcat operations in both the Middle East and Africa. These guys give outfits like ours a bad rep."

"And there's been no ransom demand?"

"None."

"What does Weston say?"

"CIA brass doesn't seem to give a rat's ass about these hostages. Weston has his sights trained purely on Laroque."

"Do you figure these hostages are somehow connected to the CIA agents' deaths?"

Jacques stilled, stared out over the inky blackness of the ocean, white foam cresting waves luminous in the moonlight. "Those mercs were hired by someone, but who? And why? And why did Laroque's men take them? Plus there's Souleyman's backing. He's getting hard cash and weaponry from some outside source that we haven't managed to identify yet. I wish to hell Carlin would make contact, because it feels like something else is going down in Ubasi, and Blake Weston doesn't give a damn."

"He's got tunnel vision. He's worried about his job. The Pentagon and the White House are putting pressure on him."

"Yeah, but if I were him, I'd be worried about a lot more."

"It's not our job to worry, Jacques."

"No, it's not. Not unless we're being played. I've got my team to think about." He glanced at Hunter. "They come first."

17:58 Zulu. Monday, November 11.
Ubasi jungle

Emily wiped thick sweat from her forehead with her sleeve, the scent of bug repellent nauseating in the sticky heat.

She and Jean had been traveling alone since daybreak, in one Jeep with three days' worth of supplies and weapons. They were moving into increasingly dense jungle in the direction of the Purple Mountains, and were now negotiating a muddy track being reclaimed by tangled growth.

Something had changed in Jean. He was terse, sullen, and she imagined she could read hostility in his eyes. His mistrust of her had deepened, she could sense it, and the farther they journeyed into thick jungle, the more vulnerable Emily felt.

He could cut her throat and dump her out here and no one would ever find her body. She'd made sure she knew the exact position of his rifle, machete and knives. Just in case.

When she'd questioned the lack of accompanying militia—especially given the size of the convoy they'd traveled with to his sister's village—he'd informed her that on that last trip they'd had information about a legitimate threat. The traitors had been dealt with. There was no immediate threat now.

He'd added that traveling into the northern jungle alone was preferable. The more quietly they moved, the less attention they'd draw to themselves. The rebels in these parts preferred a solitary visit—it was how he'd gained their confidence in the first place. "Besides," he'd said, "the jungle has eyes. Their scouts will be watching. They'll know we're coming."

That certainly didn't make her sit any easier.

She studied his rugged profile through the growing darkness, seeking some clue to his changed demeanor, until she couldn't take it anymore.

"What happened, Jean. Is it Shaka? Is he okay?"

"Yes." He wouldn't look at her. He steered their Jeep down into a water-filled pothole, spinning the tires as he edged it out the other end. His concentration was firmly ahead, his muscles too tense.

"I didn't see him in his bed in the usual place."

"He's safe."

Her stomach tightened. She hadn't seen the usual staff at the palace, either. She ducked as a branch whipped back over her head. She didn't like this. Murky blackness was closing in around the dusky yellow shafts of their headlights. Emily could no longer glimpse sky, and the growth around them seemed to develop a malevolent presence in the dark, as if watching them intently.

Another branch flung back and a thorn sliced her cheek.

She sucked in the pain, and clamped her hand down hard to stop the blood.

They were compelled to share a tent that night.

The air was soupy and their small fire belched thick, bitter-scented smoke. Laroque had fed the flames with green twigs to chase the bugs. Still, fat insects thudded against the tent fabric, sensing warm bodies inside. As the circle of firelight dwindled, so did the scope of their little world in the tangled heart of the forest.

Emily lay on lumpy ground next to Jean. Sleep was impossible. The night had come alive with a simmering orchestra of insects—a sound so loud and pervasive it seemed to have one physical shape. But if she concentrated, Emily could detect a million other little sounds layered into the composition—small clicks, groups of chirrups, rubbings, flutters, warbles, rattles, peeps, and pop-pop noises punctuated by startling screeches that echoed high in the treetops and were followed by low, aggressive warning barks.

Closer to the tent she could make out snuffles and grunts, the soft cough of an animal and an occasional crackling of twigs. Then something rustled sharply right outside their tent flap. Emily inhaled and reflexively backed up into Laroque's body.

She was shocked to find him hard. He seemed so angry, so cold and distant, yet he was aroused.

She held her breath, lay still against him, not wanting him to know she'd felt it.

Tension thickened in the smoky heat. She could hear her own heart thud until she couldn't bear his silence any longer.

"Jean?" she whispered into the darkness.

For a long time he said nothing.

Then she felt his fingernails trace the line of her neck, as if with a knife. She shuddered slightly at the mix of sensations that shivered up her spine.

A wry smile tugged at Laroque's mouth.

Her instant physical response to his slightest touch only intensified his arousal.

Why did sex with his enemy have to be the best in his life?

Thinking about it made him even hotter, harder. *Angrier.* What was he going to do with her once he had the information he needed?

Conflict churned inside him.

He touched her hair gently. It was so soft, so full, fragrant with the scent of the shampoo he'd stocked in the bathroom of the guest quarters. A bittersweetness blossomed in his chest, filling it to hurting point. He closed his eyes and nuzzled his nose into her hair, drinking in her scent as he slid his hand around to feel her breasts. Without thinking he began to undo her shirt buttons, unclasp her bra, listening to her breathing grow lighter and faster as he moved. Her breast filled his hand perfectly, her nipple hardening against his palm.

His mouth went dry. He kept his eyes closed, listening to the jungle sounds, alert to changes in the environment even as he slid his hand down her flat belly and into the front of her pants.

She sucked in air the instant he touched her between her legs, and she trembled slightly. His smile deepened. With his eyes still closed he cupped the mound between her thighs. Her slick heat brought his desire to feverish pitch. He slid a finger up into her.

She gasped lightly, opening her legs wider. Logic deserted his brain as he slipped another finger up into her, and he felt her clench her muscles around him in response, moving against him. A savage hunger surged through Laroque. He moved his fingers inside her, faster, coaxing her with small rhythmic movements, then hungry hard ones as he buried deeper inside her, and soft recurring sounds escaped her throat.

His breathing grew labored and he began to quiver against his own restraint when she suddenly arched, went stiff, swallowed a cry and shuddered, her muscles clamping down hard and spasming around his fingers. He sank his teeth into her shoulder as she climaxed again and again, until he thought he'd explode at the exquisite sensation.

Her body softened as she waited for him to move. When he did nothing, she rolled over to face him. He caught the glint of her eyes in the dark and could feel the question in her posture. She watched his face, clearly as unsure as he was about what had just happened. "Jean?" she whispered again, and he heard the vulnerability in her voice.

But when Laroque didn't answer, still didn't move, she reached for his shirt, yanked it open and kissed his chest, her lips hot, her tongue slicking his skin, teasing her way slowly toward his groin. His blood pounded. His vision turned scarlet.

He thought of the missile-homing device, of why he'd had to bring her with him into the jungle in the first place, and fury speared sharply through his belly, spearing right into the exquisite pain of his lust. He tensed, dug his fingers sharply into her thick hair and arrested her movement. There was nothing vulnerable about this woman.

She hesitated, unsure, then she opened his zipper, anyway, slid her warm fingers into his pants, exposing him. And he felt her wet, warm lips take him into her mouth. He groaned involuntarily, and reflexively tightened his grip in her hair. She began to massage him with her mouth. He sucked in his breath sharply, holding her still by the hair. *"No!"* His voice was hoarse. "No, Emma."

He had to force himself not to move against her. He wanted to ravage her, but with a ferocity that frightened him.

He pushed her quickly away, rolled out from under her touch, grabbed his rifle, unzipped the tent and stepped into the syrupy night. He pulled up his fly and forced a low and shuddering breath from deep in his chest.

His eyes burned.

He could *not* allow himself to mix rage with pleasure. He didn't want to go down that road. Ever. He point-blank refused to explore that particular combination of sensations because he was afraid he'd enjoy it—terrified he'd become his own father.

Peter Laroque had done terrible things to women in his later life. The boundaries between pain and pleasure, aggression and sex, had blurred for him.

From what Laroque had heard through the mercenary grapevine, killing had become almost orgasmic to Peter.

Laroque had even come close to slitting his own father's throat to save a woman under him. He could have—*should have*—done it, but he hadn't been able to. Instead he'd forced his father to allow the woman to crawl away for help. Then he'd withdrawn the tip of the blade from Peter's throat and walked away himself. It was shameful. And it was the last time he'd seen his father.

Laroque had been twenty years old that day. The incident haunted him still.

He'd argued endlessly with himself, that had he known just how bad Peter would become, he'd have had the courage to end his father's life that day.

When Laroque had finally heard about his father's terrible death at the hands of Congo militia, something had relaxed in him. But the news of his father's demise had not killed the fact that Peter's DNA still lurked in his body, nor the fear that the same sickness and rage could one day manifest in him.

He wiped the sweat from his face, and cursed softly.

He could not sleep with Emma now that he knew for sure she was a traitor. And what was she waiting for?

Why hadn't she stabbed him in the heart already?

She could have done it several times over, especially out here.

The uncertainty frustrated Laroque. He itched to confront her right now, get it over with. But then he might never find out who was watching her computer, who had a missile trained on his palace—

Twigs cracked suddenly in the brush.

Laroque spun, moving his weapon up in one fluid

motion. He aimed at the sound, waiting for another to come out of the blackness.

She crawled through the gap in the tent. "What was that?" she whispered.

He motioned with his head for her to stay back.

The sound moved into the night, and he lowered the gun slowly. Heart thudding.

"Jean?"

He glanced at her. She looked incredible, even out here in the jungle night, the light from the dying embers painting her face soft copper and peach. The face of a traitor, with the eyes of a sorceress. He swore again to himself.

"Have I done something?"

"Go back to sleep." He tossed a few more chunks of wood on the fire and sat on a log. "I heard something in the brush. I think I'll stay out here, keep watch."

She crawled out of the tent and came to sit beside him. He braced. Her scent was intoxicating and his pent-up desire hurt like hell. He wished she'd get back into that tent before he did something he regretted.

But they sat in heavy and uncomfortable silence as the night wore on—an hour, then another, then another.

"You asked me about my parents," she said softly.

Curiosity snaked into him. He turned his head slightly, resentfully, and listened.

Emily bit her lip.

The little details didn't matter, she told herself, the essence of what she wanted to communicate was true.

"My father was in a position of authority." She hesitated. "He was a firefighter, a fire chief," she lied.

"Was?"

She glanced at him. "He's retired." The fervor in his eyes unnerved her. "He's a charismatic and an extremely domineering man." She laughed lightly. "He's like you in a way."

He said nothing.

Emily moistened her lips. "My mother loved him with all her heart. So did—do—I. But I don't like him. My mom's entire life revolved around pleasing him, because when my dad was happy he was the most mesmerizing man around, and we adored him. He made me feel like a princess, and I suspect that's how he made my mother feel, too."

Jean leaned forward, his eyes riveted on her. But Emily no longer had the courage to meet his gaze. She barely had the grit to tell him this. She'd told no one—not flatly like this. Maybe she could do it now because she was still hiding behind an alias, because the names and professions she was using were not real. She was *still* bending the truth.

"But my dad has a very violent temper, low flashpoints, and I suspect, a pathological need to dominate the women in his life. The more my mother tried to please him over the years, the more worthless he made her feel, almost deriving pleasure from her desperation in the end." Emily inhaled deeply. "He couldn't help it. The more pathetic she got, the more it egged him on." She stared at the fire, her heart thumping. "Until one day she just…committed suicide. Killed herself. She couldn't take the rejection anymore."

Laroque remained deathly silent.

Slowly, she turned her face to him.

He was staring at her in some frightful way, conflicted emotions twisting his features.

"I was thirteen," she said. Emily tried to smile. "I lost my mom at the same age you lost yours."

He jabbed a stick at the fire, sending another cloud of orange sparks into the air. Then he sat, silently watching the flames.

"You're afraid you're like your mother?" he said without warning.

"What?"

"You're afraid you're weak, like her. You're worried that you actively seek dominant men like your father, and you're scared they'll end up controlling you. Am I right?"

She felt the blood drain from her head. "How… how do you…what makes you say that?"

"It's why you ran from me like that, after dinner, wasn't it? After I pressed you about your past. It's your dad that hurt you. He hurt you *and* your mother."

Emotion blurred her vision. Damn this man. He *could* see right through her. She turned sharply away, feeling raw, exposed.

She could feel him watching. Waiting. But she couldn't talk anymore.

"What did you do about it, Emma?"

The question surprised her. She turned slowly back to face him. "What do you mean?"

"How did you fight back? Did you talk to him?"

She swallowed. She hadn't ever had the courage to tell her dad that she thought her mum's death was his fault. And here *she* was the shrink. Guilt deepened in her.

"I studied psychology," she said, leaving out the army bit. "That was my way of fighting back. I needed the tools to understand men like him, and society's relationship to them."

"Do you?"

"Yes," she said, staring at the fire. "Yes, I do. I've become something of an expert in the field."

"But it doesn't change, does it? How you feel *inside?*"

Her eyes flicked to him in surprise. "No," she said. "It doesn't."

He swore bitterly.

She frowned at him. "What was that for?"

His eyes narrowed. "You and me, we're one of a kind."

"What do you mean?"

"You understand *me,* don't you?" Anger shimmered over his features, tightened his neck.

"I think I understand *some* of your conflict, Jean, about who you are. Your fear. I understand your need to belong. Your need for family."

Angrily, he lurched to his feet and cast another log into the fire, sending a scattering of small orange sparks into the blackness. He glared at her, then stalked around to the far end of their encampment.

They might be one of a kind, but right now they were on opposite sides of the battle fence.

He spun back to face her suddenly, the shadows hiding his features. "Why are you telling me this *now,* Emma?"

"Because…I needed to, Jean."

She needed him to know she cared enough to share this deeply personal part of herself, even though she couldn't tell him who she was.

She'd felt him retreating further and further from her the deeper into the jungle they'd traveled. He hadn't even been able to commit to making love to her properly in the tent, and it had left a hollowness in her stomach.

And in her heart.

She wanted him to like *her*—Emily. She wanted to try and connect with him on some deeper level, yet she was compelled not to blow her cover, or the FDS mission.

It was more than just her life at stake.

There were the lives of Jacques's men to think of.

21:19 Zulu. Tuesday, November 12.
Rebel camp. Northern Ubasi jungle

Laroque and the rebels conversed in turbulent tones around a large campfire. Ebony faces glistened with sweat, the whites of eyes flashed, muscles in cutoff shirts flexed—the men were agitated, aggressive.

Emily couldn't make out a single word of the dialect they used. The mood, however, was clear. These men spoke with a provocative anger.

Every now and then one would launch to his feet and yell something, his finger pointing at Laroque, muscles cording in powerful arms. She watched quietly from the darkness, captivated, as Laroque raised his hand in quiet authority, his response measured, unquestionably firm, brooking no argument.

He was undeniably the leader of this wild bunch, a respected power figure in a group of rough warriors. Le Diable's strength was elegant, his sharp eyes cool with shrewd intelligence. Yet his physical resonance matched the raw strength of each of these men.

Emily edged back into the shadows. She waited for a few moments, but no one seemed to have noticed her move. She backed farther out of their line of sight. Still no one looked her way.

She quickly surveyed her surroundings.

The compound was not big, and she'd seen where Laroque had been taken to interrogate the captives. She'd also counted every one of the militants as she'd moved around the compound earlier. They were all accounted for around the fire.

Her pulse raced. This was her chance.

She made her way across the compound quietly, halting every few steps to see if she was being followed, listening for a change in timbre or tempo of the voices around the fire. From Laroque's Jeep she quickly retrieved a flashlight and a knife, which she slid into the top of her boot underneath her pants.

She made her way along a narrow path, well screened from the fire by brush. She wondered why they'd left the small lean-to that housed the prisoners unguarded as she peered through the uneven slats of wood. The stench was awful, and she could see nothing but darkness.

"Hello?" she whispered. "Anyone in there?"

Dead silence greeted her.

She hesitated, glanced over her shoulder. She was taking one hell of a chance, but these hostages were somehow key to what was happening in Ubasi. She needed to try to talk to them, find out who they were, and why Laroque's men had captured them. She'd come up with an excuse if caught.

The lock on the door hung open. She figured she knew why—the men were either dead or close to it.

She also knew they had been alive *before* Laroque got to them.

Dreading what she would see, Emily carefully edged open the door.

Chapter 12

22:37 Zulu. Tuesday, November 12.
Rebel camp. Northern Ubasi jungle

She froze, heart thudding, waiting for the sound of voices. None came. The night sounds were cloaking her movements.

Emily carefully directed her flashlight into the shack. A black-and-yellow striped snake the length of a fishing rod slithered along the dirt floor, trying to escape her beam. She counted her breaths, waiting for it to leave, and then she slowly panned the inside of the tiny building with her light.

She could make out four men huddled against one another in the corner. They were so beaten and bloodied she could barely distinguish features or race. Her stomach tightened, and she moved rapidly forward.

She crouched down in front of one man. His eyes were swollen shut. She touched his arm gently and he groaned, trying to shrink back. "Shh, it's okay," she whispered. "You can trust me." His skin was burning hot. He was running a raging fever. She figured this was one of the Nigerian nationals. She quickly scanned the others with her beam of light. They were in no better condition. They *were* more fair. One looked like his hair might once have been blond under the dirt and blood; the other two were brown-haired.

She couldn't find the fifth man.

Then she saw black boots sticking out from under a pile of old sacks. She touched the pile and flies rose in a cloud. Her stomach lurched.

What had they done to these men?

"Are you American?" she whispered to one as she carefully tried to removed the ragged cloth that gagged him.

He groaned, nodded slightly.

"They tortured you?"

He nodded, unable to speak.

"Did…did Jean-Charles Laroque do any of this to you?" She *had* to know.

He appeared confused. These men were all dying and Emily didn't know how to help.

"Le Diable," she whispered. "Did *he* hurt you?"

The man murmured something through his swollen lips, and nodded.

Inexplicable disappointment sunk through Emily. She leaned closer. "I can get help for you. Can you tell me who you are?"

His hand gripped hers suddenly, fingers digging with desperation into her skin. "Promise…" He groaned in pain. "Promise me…"

Emily leaned closer, urgency nipping at her. "Promise *what?*" she whispered.

"My…son. I…told him I'd be home…Thanks- giving. Must promise me, please…get home to…my boy for Thanksgiving."

Her heart buckled. "Where's home?"

"Oklahoma…home—" he croaked, blood leak- ing from the corner of his cracked mouth "—that's my…home."

Emily closed her eyes for a moment, holding back a shudder of emotion. There was no way in hell this man was ever going to see home again. She knelt closer, smoothed his hair back from his feverish forehead. "Tell me," she whispered. "Tell me why they brought you here."

14:00 Zulu. Thursday, November 14.
Ubasi jungle

"What's going to happen to the hostages?" Emily had to shout over the whine of the Jeep.

He continued to ignore her as he floored the gas, hitting a pothole with bone-jarring force. Emily ducked as vines whipped past her face. He'd been driving like this—belligerently and recklessly—for the past twenty-fours, and it was sending her clean over the edge.

"Dammit, Jean!" she yelled in frustration. "You dragged me all this way! The *least* you can do is *say* something!"

He slammed on the brakes suddenly and she flew forward, striking the dashboard with such force it knocked the air from her.

He whirled to face her, eyes glinting with green fire. "Do you think I don't know you went in there, Emma?"

She felt her jaw drop.

"You sneaked in behind my back to see those captives, didn't you?"

Her chest tightened. She was suddenly afraid to speak, threatened by the hawkish glint in his eyes. She edged her hand slowly along the side of the Jeep, ready to find purchase if she needed to scramble out and run for her life into the forest, knowing at the same time she'd never survive a night on her own in this place.

"Do you think I don't know what those men told you?"

She tried to moisten her bone-dry mouth. "You… spied on me?"

He barked a harsh laugh. *"Spy!* What the hell do you think *you* were doing if not *spying?"*

Her cheeks went hot. "You set me up. You specifically waited for me to go there."

He lowered his voice further, glacial eyes cleaving

into hers. "Why did you do it, Emma? Why are you spying on me?" His voice was dangerously level, quiet.

She glanced away, trying to gather herself, scrambling for words. She'd so desperately wanted to believe everything he'd told her, but after seeing those men, she couldn't. And it had *broken* something inside her, to think he'd done that to innocent men with families back home. It had hardened her resolve to fulfill her mission, but it had also filled her heart with pain.

"*Why,* Emma?"

She turned slowly to face him, her eyes moistening. "Because…they're my fellow citizens, Jean," she said. "I couldn't just sit there and do nothing. I *had* to see them. I…" She looked down at her hands. "They're hurt, Jean." Her eyes flashed up. "*You* hurt them."

His eyes burned into her, and a small muscle pulsed rapidly at his jaw. "You're lying to me, Emma."

She swallowed. "It's the truth."

"Give me the knife."

Her eyes flickered. "What…knife?"

"The knife in your boot, dammit. *My* knife."

She sat motionless. He waited, his eyes locked onto hers. She slowly extracted the hunting blade she'd taken and held it out to him.

He took it, unsheathed it, held the gleaming hooked tip in front of her face. Emily stared at it, adrenaline surging into her blood, the fight or flight impulses warring inside her. She couldn't breathe.

"And what were you doing with *this?*"

She didn't dare swallow, let alone speak, for fear he'd kill her.

"What *else* have you taken from me, Emma?"

The blade glinted, catching light as he twisted it, and his eyes lanced hers. In them she could read not only rage, but disappointment, pain. And that hurt Emily more than anything. He seemed to be fighting with his emotions, struggling against something. He pulled back suddenly and thrust the knife into a pocket of the door with a hard thud.

Her eyes watered with relief and she covered her throat with her hands, heart slamming wildly.

He glared at the dirt track ahead. "Whatever those men told you, Emma, they lied."

The residual effects of adrenaline made her begin to shake. She wanted to cry. She was so damn conflicted she didn't know what to do. "Those men weren't lying, Jean." Her voice came out hoarse, wobbly. "They were *beyond* lying. One man is a father. He just wants to get home to his family for Thanksgiving. He works security for a mine in Nigeria, and he was due to go home when your men took them. I have no idea why you wanted them, but whoever you thought they were…they're innocent."

He laughed dryly.

Anger began to pull at Emily's mouth. She tried to control herself, tried to tell herself to shut up, but she had virtually nothing to lose now. The FDS and Souleyman's men would be storming the castle in less than ten hours, and Jean would be dead.

"Those men have been hurt," she said quietly. "They need help. They are not going to survive more than a day or so in this climate with wounds like that. They'll be dead before tomorrow, if they aren't already."

He whipped his eyes to hers. "You actually believe *them* over me?"

Her jaw tightened. "Tell me why you took them, Jean."

"Why should I?"

So that I can pick a damn side!

She dropped her face into her hands. It was no use. She had no idea what to believe anymore.

"They knew the game, Emma."

She looked up sharply. "What do you mean?"

"They went in knowing the risks. Do *you* know the risks?"

She felt the blood drain from her face. "What are you implying?"

He started the Jeep, shunted it into gear and began to drive. Frustration exploded in her. "You're no better than Souleyman, you know that!"

He slammed on the brakes and spun round, ice in his eyes. "Don't you *ever* compare me to that man," he growled through clenched teeth, stark white against the dark anger in his face.

"Why *not?*" she said, holding his gaze. "Why is it right for you to hurt innocent people like those hostages? How is that any different from Souleyman hurting your sister for his own political gain?"

"Those men," he said, "are not oil workers.

They're mercenaries. They signed up for this. My sister *didn't*. Those men don't give a damn who they kill, or what they destroy, because when they pick up guns, they do it solely for the cash."

"Mercenaries?"

He watched her struggle with the notion. "Yes, and they lied to you, Emma, because they thought the lies might save them."

"I…who're they working for, then? What…what did they do? Why did you take them?"

"They killed those four American geologists."

The CIA agents?

Her jaw dropped. "What?"

"That's right. Do you feel so sorry for them now?"

"I…don't believe you."

He snorted as if she was no longer worth wasting precious time on. Slamming the Jeep back into gear, he hit the gas and they swerved forward into red mud.

Emily literally shook with adrenaline. Could it possibly be true? Did Jean actually *know* the geologists were CIA agents? Had his suspicions—that someone paid mercenaries to kill the agents in a way that would set Jean up to take the fall—been right all along?

And here she was, part of Washington's initiative—a pawn sent to destroy him, her own people backing Souleyman.

The cloak and daggers of this game were confounding.

She felt sick.

She had to get word to Jacques. This could change everything.

She stared at Laroque's rugged profile, and her heart swelled with pain and emotion. He looked so alone. And she didn't know if she should believe him—and help him.

She had no idea what side to step down on, yet the clock was ticking fast. If she did nothing, he would be killed in under ten hours.

Tension ratcheted in her stomach. Even if she wanted to help him, the only way to do it now would be to come clean, tell him who she worked for, so that he'd allow her to access her communications systems.

That would mean losing him—forever. This was not the kind of man to take betrayal lightly.

She'd seen what happened to the soldier who'd deceived him.

And coming clean would mean blowing a Pentagon-CIA initiative. She had to be *damn* sure that what her gut was telling her was right.

Laroque swerved into the castle courtyard and screeched to a halt, his heart racing. Under torture, the so-called hostages had confessed they were freelance fighters contracted by a covert arm of the Chinese government. This covert and renegade faction of the ruling Chinese communist party had tried to frame Laroque and force him into a deadly confrontation with Washington. In the meantime, the

Chinese were backing Souleyman in a bid to over-throw Laroque and take Ubasi, and Souleyman's men were mobilizing for attack this very minute.

Laroque did not have a moment to lose if he wanted to save his country.

In return for military aid and substantial funding, Souleyman had promised the Chinese sole access to the Ubasi oil reserves. The Chinese also wanted to nip Laroque's oil cartel in the bud.

Laroque's sole intent now was to find out who Emma Sanford was working for—the Chinese or someone else—and her computer was going to tell him.

Almost immediately, he saw Mano motioning urgently to him from the far end of the courtyard. Laroque raised two fingers in acknowledgment as he swung his legs over the side of the Jeep.

Emma scrambled out, hesitated, uncertainty in her eyes. "Jean—"

"Make sure she goes directly to her room," he commanded his guards, cutting her off. "Bolt her in."

Shock and fear rippled over her features as his men took her by the arms.

"Jean, wait!"

"Take her. Now."

He watched them go. He saw the determination in the set of her shoulders, then, suddenly, a flash of vulnerability. He clenched his fists. He could use a woman like her on his side. He *wanted* her at his side. He wanted her in his bed. He simply wanted her.

But she wasn't Emma. And she stood against him…he *couldn't* let her get in his way.

Then, before he even knew what he was doing, he yelled after her. "I didn't touch them!"

She stopped and slowly turned round, the sun catching her eyes.

"I did not touch those hostages, Emma."

She held his eyes for a long beat, guards waiting on either side. Then she spun away and entered his castle, his guards escorting her.

Laroque palmed off his beret and dragged his hand over his hair. He didn't know what the hell had compelled him to say that. *Especially* with his men watching.

But he needed her to know that he hadn't beaten those men himself.

His mouth turned bitter.

One of these days his men were going to call him on this sort of thing. They were going to see that his bark was worse than his bite, that he didn't physically have it in him to kill a man—or woman—who wasn't fighting him squarely back on even terms.

Laroque liked a challenge. But he was not an abuser of power.

He liked to win fair.

The trouble was, if he wanted to hold on to his power and keep the respect of his army—especially men like those rebels in the north—he was going to need to be seen meting out swift punishment to those who committed treason, or betrayal.

And that included Emma.

Whether she was working for the Chinese or someone else, he was going to have to act. And ruthlessly so.

Justice in this land tended to be harsh. It's what people expected, because the land itself was harsh.

As she disappeared up the castle stairs, flanked by his guards, her hair catching the last rays of the evening sun, Mano approached him.

"We've set her up, Jean."

He nodded.

"All she has to do is start typing."

"Let's do it, then," he said. "We have no time to waste."

But as Laroque marched across the courtyard, he found himself praying that somehow, he'd still find her innocent.

That he wouldn't be put to the test.

17:03 Zulu. Thursday, November 14.
Ubasi Palace

The guards unlocked the door to her suite, and Emily stepped in—and stilled instantly.

Her computer lay on the bed.

She stared at it, anxiety ripping through her. The bolt slid into place behind her, and she waited until the echo of the guards' boots faded down the corridor before walking slowly over to the bed to examine the laptop.

It was definitely her system.

Sweat prickled over her skin.

Jean was on to her. She'd felt it as they'd headed into the jungle. Known it for certain when she'd badgered him about the hostages. Now this. What game was he playing now?

Emily rubbed her hand over her brow as she stared at the computer—her only link to the outside world.

She glanced up at the clock. Jacques's men would be moving in less than nine hours.

She began to pace the room, trying to think.

Jean obviously didn't know *exactly* who she was, because he would have done something about it. He must, however, have found solid reason to mistrust her—in her computer. And now he was setting her up.

Emily swore softly, sat on the bed, picked up her laptop and turned it over, trying to see if he'd tampered with it.

She could just forget the damn computer. Do nothing.

She'd be okay in the castle. Jacques's men would find her here. She pushed a lock of damp hair off her face. The FDS would storm the palace with Souleyman's men. They'd take Jean down. Kill him.

She jerked to her feet, began to pace again.

Ubasi would be a dead zone under Souleyman. She couldn't let that happen. And she could *not* let them assassinate Jean-Charles Laroque—not if he was innocent of killing those CIA agents, not if what he'd said about forming a cartel was true. It would be plain wrong.

Never mind her own attraction to Jean.

And in spite of what Washington or the other superpowers of the world might want, she believed a cartel that saw oil profits benefit the indigenous populations would be a good thing.

If the United States was using her and the FDS as pawns in a bid to stop a cartel forming in the Gulf of Guinea, she had to take a stand against it.

Who would she be if she didn't?

She pressed her hand against her stomach, trying to quell the nerves.

She'd seen what Jean was trying to protect, to build in this country. The more she thought about it, the more she believed he was telling the truth.

She didn't yet understand how the hostages fitted in, or who might have paid them to kill the CIA agents, but it was her duty to inform Jacques about what she'd seen and heard. Jacques's men *needed* to know what they were up against, that things were not what they seemed in Ubasi.

And regardless of her personal feelings, her mission was to deliver a psychological assessment of *Le Diable*.

She *had* to use the computer.

Emily stared at it, anxiety and adrenaline warring in her body, sweat totally drenching her shirt.

She pulled her hair back with both hands. If she risked using the laptop, and Jean was monitoring her, she'd tip him off to Jacques's men. She could be placing her own FDS colleagues directly in the line of fire.

She could be endangering their lives and her own

while single-handedly scuttling a CIA-Pentagon initiative.

But if she *didn't* take action, and he was killed, and his dream of an independent Ubasi was destroyed, she'd be tormented for the rest of her life over her decision. She'd be liable for perpetuating foreign policies she could no longer believe in.

Whose lives weighed more? And who the hell was she to judge?

God, she was in an impossible bind.

Emily plunked herself down onto the bed and buried her face in her hands. She had to trust her heart, that's all she could do.

And her heart was telling her that she'd been falling in love with Jean-Charles Laroque every step of the way.

And that she was compelled to save him—and his dream.

But if she touched that computer, she was going to lose him forever. He would see firsthand that she had betrayed him in the most intimate fashion.

But if she didn't touch it…emotion burned in her chest.

Emily's eyes flicked toward the clock, and the belt of tension tightened another notch over her stomach. She was running out of time.

She had to do it. Now. Suffer any consequence. And if she ever got out of this alive, Emily vowed she would not look back. Ever. She'd just let go of Jean and all the mistakes she'd ever made. She'd move forward, make some serious changes in her life and work toward something positive. Something fresh.

She sucked in a deep breath, opened the laptop, closed her eyes for a second, steadying her mind, then started it up, typing in the code that would activate the signal and relay her words directly to the monitors on São Diogo Island.

17:20 Zulu. Thursday, November 14.
Communications room. FDS Base, São Diogo Island

The monitor flashed a steady alert signal, then crackled softly to life. Code started to move rapidly across the screen. April Ngomo's heart slammed against her rib cage. She lurched across the desk, hit the button that sounded the alarm in Jacques's office.

Relief gushed through Jacques as he raced to the communications room. Damn, he'd been worried about Emily Carlin. He flung open the door just in time to see her first sentence appearing on the large LCD screen above April's desk.

"Been to see hostages. Four still alive. Need medical attention ASAP. Laroque claims they are mercenaries responsible for CIA deaths. Being held in rebel camp in Purple foothills just west of laptop GPS coordinates. I'm safe, being held at palace..."

Jacques glanced quickly at the green GPS signal on the other monitor. It had moved within the palace for the first time in days. He whipped his eyes back to the main screen, conscious of Hunter entering the room behind him.

"Laroque would not make cooperative captive in my assessment. Capture would ensure martyrdom status. But situ—" The screen suddenly went dead.

Jacques's heart plummeted.

Everyone in the room sat silent for a moment, staring at the blank screen.

Jacques shot a look at April. "What happened?"

"Someone cut her off!" said April, spinning back to her keyboard and quickly entering a series of codes. "She didn't sign out. Someone's tracking *us*…" She rapidly hit more keys. "Damn, I can't track back."

"What do you mean?" asked Jacques, moving quickly to her side.

"I mean, they've hacked into her system! They saw what we just saw up on that monitor." She pointed. "They're on to us. They're on to her. She's in trouble!"

"We move. Now." Jacques spun round. "Give the orders to mobilize ASAP. Code Green."

That was the code to assassinate Laroque at first opportunity.

"You sure, Jacques?" Hunter sounded skeptical.

"As sure as I can be."

Hunter stepped forward, kept his voice low. "There's a *'but'* in that message. It looked as though Carlin was going to add some sort of qualifier."

"It doesn't matter," said Jacques. "We don't have time to second-guess her. Carlin's job was to make that one assessment. She has. And she's given us the coordinates for the mercs."

"That's not part of *our* job."

"No. It's not. But she said it herself, those hostages are mercs and could be linked to the CIA deaths. It's consistent with what we dug up on them. Something else is going down here, and like it or not, we've been engaged. We're going after those prisoners—and Laroque."

17:20 Zulu. Thursday, November 14.
Communications room. Ubasi Palace

Mano shot his hand into the air. "She's in!"

Laroque spun to face the monitor. A grave silence filled the room.

Code began to appear on the screen. Mano motioned quickly for his techs to start triangulating. Seconds clicked on the clock. She needed to stay on her system for twenty seconds minimum to get an accurate reading on the coordinates.

Laroque's eyes locked onto the letters as they appeared. She began to type fast, and his chest tightened.

"Been to see hostages. Four still alive. Need…"

He flicked his eyes briefly to the clock, back to the text.

"…medical attention ASAP. Laroque claims they are mercenaries responsible for CIA deaths. Being held in rebel camp in Purple foothills just west of laptop GPS coordinates. I'm safe, being held at palace…"

The bitter taste of betrayal leached up the back of his throat.

"Laroque would not make cooperative captive in my assessment..."

His hands fisted. It was so damned personal. A desecration.

"...Capture would ensure martyrdom..."

"Got it! We got a GPS reading!"

"Kill it!" Laroque barked to the techs.

"...status. But the situ—"

"Now, goddammit! Stop that thing!"

The screen went blank. He was breathing hard. Sweating. Shaking inside.

"Where are they?" he said, his neck muscles bunched so tight he could barely squeeze the words out.

Mano rapidly hit a few keys, and the global positioning coordinates came up. A map enlarged, crosshairs zeroing in to a small island.

"There!" Mano pointed. "São Diogo Island, off the Angolan coast."

Laroque stared blindly at the blatant proof of her deceit mocking him from the screen, ripping him apart from the inside out. His nails bit into his palms as he clenched his fists in a struggle to restrain the rawness of his emotion, to digest what she'd done to him.

This was it.

He *had* to face the test.

He knew that every man in the room had their eyes trained on him at this very moment. He was their leader. And they waited to see what he'd do to the woman who'd come to destroy their country.

The woman who had made love to him with such tenderness in her eyes that he had dared dream of a future.

Now she was taking it all. And he'd made it possible by allowing himself to be played for a fool.

He could not let her win. He would *not* let her take him down.

He clenched his teeth, spun on his heels and barked a command to his men.

They reached for their weapons and followed him down the corridor, toward her room.

17:20 Zulu. Thursday, November 14.
Guest suite. Ubasi Palace

Emily froze as the screen suddenly went stone-cold dead.

Her heart started to thud. She quickly tried to reboot, reenter her code, type again. Nothing worked.

Panic shot through her as she heard several sets of boots thundering down the corridor toward her room. She heard a barked command.

Laroque's voice!

Her bedroom door smashed open and cracked back against the wall.

Laroque filled the door frame, fury twisting his features, the agony of betrayal burning in his eyes.

Chapter 13

Laroque stepped up to her, toe-to-toe, forcing her to look up and expose the smooth column of her neck. His men guarded the door with their rifles and bayonets.

"Who *are* you?" he asked.

Her eyes flicked to the guards, the weapons. Her features were taut with distress, perspiration drenching her shirt.

"Jean, please…I can explain. I—"

He raised his hand to silence her. "I want your name, your *real* name." It was the only question he wanted answered.

Laroque had a burning need to know who he had fallen for, who had betrayed him in this most intimate fashion, cracking through his emotional armor, exposing the intensely personal and private part of his heart.

Who was this woman who'd come so very close to destroying his dream for Ubasi?

She swallowed, and tears filled her eyes. "Emily," she said, very softly. "My name is Dr. Emily Carlin."

Laroque's chest burned as he looked into those glistening violet eyes. "You *are* a doctor?"

She nodded. "A psychologist."

A strange wave of relief surged through Laroque. He couldn't explain why. Perhaps it was because her name was so close to her alias. Perhaps it was because parts of her *were* real. But it was small comfort.

"Who are you working for?"

"The Force du Sable."

He swore. The mercenary world was an incredibly small one. The FDS was a known outfit based off the coast of Angola. Her information jibed with coordinates Mano had just triangulated. "Who are *they* working for?" he demanded.

She looked away sharply.

Aware that his men were watching, he grabbed her chin, twisting her head back to face him. "Answer me. And don't try to lie to me, Dr. Carlin. It won't help you," he said, holding her chin firmly.

"Jean, please—"

"Who!"

She swallowed. "The United States."

His stomach muscles tightened. "You've made contact with your people. What is their plan now?"

"I…I'm so sorry, Jean." The moisture escaped her eyes and trickled down her cheeks.

He swore bitterly. "Don't feed me that line. At least do me *that* justice. Tell me what to expect."

Emily closed her eyes, and inhaled a shuddering breath. "They'll attack," she said, looking slowly back up at him. "They'll be mobilizing now. They're backing Souleyman."

Disappointment smacked hard. "A coup?"

She nodded.

"Fools!" He spat the word at her. "You thought you were doing me in, didn't you?" He backed away from her. "But you're just screwing yourselves, do you know that?"

She winced. "It wasn't like that, Jean."

"What the hell was it, then? Jesus, Emma, you made me *care!*"

"Emily," she whispered.

"Right. I fell for someone who doesn't exist." He fingered the knife hilt in the sheath at his hip, and her eyes nervously tracked his movement.

"If your FDS friends and the Pentagon are backing Souleyman, they're in for one hell of a rude awakening, Dr. Carlin."

"Why?" she asked softly.

He snorted. "Because he's a two-timing, double-crossing sonofabitch, that's why. He's in bed with someone else already."

Her eyes flared. "*Who* else?" she whispered.

"Those mercenaries you so desperately wanted to

save? They were hired by a Chinese organization linked all the way up to Beijing. You see, *Emily,* it's not only the United States who wants access to Ubasi oil. The Chinese want it, too. And they've backed Souleyman to the hilt in a deal to get it—all of it— because they sure as hell knew they weren't going to get it from me. *They* paid those mercenaries to slaughter and gut your CIA agents."

Blood drained from her face. *"Oh my God."*

"That surprises you, does it, Dr. Carlin? Those dead CIA agents discovered that this covert arm of the Beijing government had been working behind the scenes to undermine U.S. interests in the Gulf, and the Chinese couldn't afford to let that secret out. Not while Beijing is in sensitive trade negotiations with Washington and playing all nice at the diplomatic table. They had to get rid of those agents fast, and make it look like someone else did it, or they were going to have a nice neo-Cold War on their hands."

"So they framed you."

"Why not? Everyone else thinks I'm the bad guy. Their hope was that when Souleyman finally killed me off, their secret would die with me, and the U.S. would come looking no further. My death would end the cartel that would have restricted China's oil access."

He barked a harsh laugh. "Bet they didn't count on *your* friends actually helping give Souleyman a leg up. He's going to turn around and stab your FDS buddies in the back as soon as he has my head on a stick."

"How…how do you *know* this?"

"That dead man you saw in that shack? The other hostages didn't want to end up like him. They spilled their guts to my men. Those mercs hold no allegiance to anything other than cash. They weren't going to die for a secret Chinese organization."

"Jean…I…I had no idea—"

He came up close to her, bent his head low, bringing his mouth alongside her ear so that his men couldn't hear. "I should have known better than hope you were for real, Emily Carlin," he whispered against her ear. "I thought I could love you." She shuddered, and her tear-filled eyes flashed wide to his. Her lips were so close to his that he felt the familiar, deceptive jolt to the groin. He clenched his jaw. "You are the worst kind of enemy, you know that?" he murmured through gritted teeth, almost touching her cheek with his lips.

Then he jerked back sharply and turned to his guards.

"Take her to the dungeons!"

The guards stepped in and grabbed her by the arms. She strained against them. *"Jean!"* But he turned away, he couldn't bear to look at her. He couldn't bear the pain.

"Wait, Jean!"

He walked toward the door.

"Wait, please, for God's sake. Just listen to me! They *will* kill you!"

He stopped in the doorway, then turned slowly to face her. "That was your plan, wasn't it? To assess whether I was worthy of capture, or death?"

"No…yes…I mean—"

He left.

"Jean, dammit! Wait!"

He kept on walking down the passage.

"Jean! I can help you! I…I can save you if you just let me speak to the FDS. Jean! I *believe* in you. I…I *care* for you, too, dammit! What we shared—that was *real!*"

He stood stone-still. His hands fisted at his sides. He swallowed, forcing himself not to look back.

He did not want to hear another word from her traitorous mouth. The desperation was from fear for herself and her own team now. This was a calculating woman who'd slept with him in order to get into his mind. She was not above saying this now, of hurting him in the deepest way possible. If only she knew just how much he'd wished for her to be someone else.

He inhaled sharply, shoring his anger, and he walked away without looking. He didn't have a moment to lose now. He was at war.

"Evacuate the palace!" he ordered his men as he stalked down the passage. "Go to ground. Plan delta."

"What about the woman?"

He hesitated briefly. "The safest place is the dungeons. It's designed as a bomb shelter."

He saw the quick exchange of glances. He knew his men wanted her executed, and soon. She was a curse to them. To their country. *To him.* And they were going to see his failure to swiftly deal with her as a weakness.

But as deeply as Emily Carlin had hurt him, as close as she'd come to bringing him and his country down, it wasn't in Laroque to hurt the woman he loved.

Even if her betrayal could be his downfall.

Emily huddled in the corner of her dank cell. There were no windows or electricity down in the dungeons. Rusting manacles still hung from chains bolted to the stone walls, thick with mold and years of grime. This place had been built at the time of the Crusades and had not changed since.

But she didn't give a damn about herself now. She had to find a way to warn Jacques about Souleyman and the Chinese, and she had to do it soon.

His men would be mobilizing, sparked by her prematurely truncated message. And they'd have gotten the wrong idea about Jean.

She'd been about to type that although Jean was not a good candidate for capture, she believed he was doing good, and that the coup must be stopped.

God, if only he'd let her type long enough he would have seen for himself that she was on his side now. She was on both sides. Jean *had* to see that. The FDS could be his best ally now. She could be his only hope.

Emily stood on tiptoe and tried to peer through the bars of the iron door on her cell. She could make out a guard standing near a torch farther along the dark corridor. "Hey! Hello there! Hey!" she yelled as she banged on the door, trying to get the guard's attention.

He glanced her way and her heart raced.

"Help me, please!" She banged on the door in desperation. "Please!"

He didn't move, but she could see that she'd snared his interest.

"Please, come here. You *must* listen to me. Laroque—Le Diable—your leader, he is in danger. His *life* is in danger!"

Desperation choked Emily. Her eyes filled with hot emotion. *"Please."*

He must have heard the sheer anguish in her voice, because he edged closer, curious.

"Look, just come here and listen to me. I can't do anything to you. But *you* could do something. You could save Le Diable. You could save Ubasi. Just hear me out, please."

He hesitated, then swung his AK round in front of him, and walked over to her cell, stopping a short distance away.

"Ask him to come down here, please. I have information that will enable him to stop the attack on Ubasi. But it can't wait. I must speak to him now. In a few more minutes it will be too late."

The guard studied her, suspicion in his eyes.

She tried to steady her voice as she gripped tighter on the bars. "It can do no harm for him to come, can it?" she said softly, tears starting to spill down her cheeks. "But it would save his life. I promise you that."

Hesitation rippled through the young man's features. He didn't like her, Emily could see that. But she had to count on the fact that this soldier revered his leader. Without Laroque, he was not going to have a future in Ubasi.

"You could be a hero," she said softly. "For your country."

His eyes narrowed sharply, then he turned and walked away.

Emily sank down into a limp pile behind the iron door and buried her head against her knees. She rocked her body, tears streaming silently down her face.

She'd failed.

Chapter 14

"I apologize if I am wrong, but I thought it best I alert you, sir."

Laroque studied the earnest young guard's face and he couldn't help thinking of himself at that age, fighting his father's brutal wars. It was not something he'd wish on anyone. This man still had a chance. It was young men like him who were Ubasi's future. Laroque owed it to him not to ignore any hope at peaceful resolution. No matter how small.

He went down to her cell.

He heard her out without looking at her even once, and then he'd had her brought in handcuffs up to the communications room. He still could not look at her.

He motioned to Mano to take over. "Take the cuffs off. Give her whatever she needs."

Mano quickly set up a communications link with Jacques Sauvage at the FDS base, and offered Emily a seat in front of the terminal.

Laroque would have left her to it, but he had to hear what she said to the FDS. He needed to be in a position to stop her if he suspected foul play.

But just being in the same room as her was painful.

"Jean?" she said, before taking her seat in front of the terminal. The soft hesitation, the broken spirit in her voice, ripped through him, but he forced himself to remain cold. But inside he burned—with betrayal, with unspent passion for her.

"Jean, I…I meant what I said. When I—"

"Just contact your damn people," he growled through clenched teeth. "Then leave me the hell alone."

23:58 Zulu. Thursday, November 14.
FDS Base, São Diogo Island

Jacques signed off. Carlin's news worked through his brain, all the little disjointed pieces that had been nagging at him slotting fast and cleanly into place.

He trusted she was not speaking under duress. They had code for that. And what she had just told him about Souleyman, while shattering, added up. They had to move fast now. Blake Weston was not going to like this, but he'd change his mind pretty damn quick when he learned about the alleged Chinese involvement.

If Beijing really was behind the scenes, the U.S. could be facing a neo-Cold War era—especially given China's recently demonstrated antisatellite capabilities. This could shape up to be a race not only to secure world energy resources and control of space but global military domination, especially given the recent strengthening of Sino-Russian ties.

Jacques reached for the communications console and flicked a switch. "Change of plan. Call off Code Green. I repeat, terminate Code Green…." Then he barked a series of orders to his men with his classic machine-gun precision.

00:02 Zulu. Friday, November 15.
Communications room, Ubasi Palace

Emily rubbed her wrists where the handcuffs had chafed her skin, but it was a different kind of pain she needed to assuage. She ached to touch Jean just one more time, just to have him look her in the eyes again. But he'd shut her out.

He stood like a towering hunk of cold granite, his back to her, waiting for her to leave the room.

"Jean, please look at me."

He stood silent for a long time, and then walked slowly from the room, leaving a hollow in her stomach.

He didn't close the door. He didn't say not to follow him, either. It was almost as if he needed to see that she would dare come after him now that her job here was done.

She did.

She found him in his private quarters, which commanded a startling view of the jungle canopy all the way to the Purple Mountains. But dawn was still hours away and the night was dark and oppressive, the air charged with the pressure and electricity of a coming storm. Emily could hear choppers, faint in the distance, cutting over the black canopy from Cameroon—Jacques's men coming to get her. The tall palms outside rattled their leaves in the gusts of hot, mounting wind.

He stood staring out the arched stone windows into the blackness as the breeze billowed over his cotton shirt and lifted his hair. Emily approached softly behind him.

She hesitated, unsure of what to say, how close to go. She reached out to touch him, almost finding words, but she was so conflicted and confused about where to go from here that she was virtually paralyzed. She dropped her hand back to her side.

He broke the silence, speaking into the distance.

"She said a woman with eyes the same color as the hills out there would be my downfall."

Surprise shimmered through her. "Who said that?"

"The Ubasi high priestess," he said, without looking at her. "I never listened, didn't even remember her words, until my men reminded me." He remained silent a long time. "I should have listened."

"You don't believe in that stuff, Jean."

"I don't. But my people do. Souleyman used your

arrival as a sign. He started the rumor that you were the temptress of the prophecy, and when Souleyman said I was growing weak because of you, that's when I felt something change in my men." He paused. "Or maybe it was me that changed. Because you *did* make me weak. I allowed your hold over me to jeopardize my dream." He snorted softly, still refusing to look at her. "Maybe it *is* true. Maybe there are such things." He was silent. "Maybe it's over."

A strange chill brushed her skin "What exactly did the priestess say?"

"That I would hold power until a woman with eyes the color of the Purple Mountains arrived and changed everything."

"She didn't say you'd lose power."

"Doesn't matter. I never wanted to rule. I did this job for the king, and for my sister. I did it for my country." He paused. "And it is my country. It's become my home."

"The king?"

"He hired me to take Ubasi. He paid me in oil exploration blocks."

"Where is he?" she asked, bewildered.

"Doesn't matter. Not to you."

Hurt pinged through her. "Change doesn't mean downfall, Jean. Change—the end of something— usually signals rebirth."

He was quiet for a moment. "I'd like you to leave."

She touched his shoulder and he tensed like wire under her fingertips. "I meant what I said, Jean.

I...I don't think I've ever felt this way about another man. I—"

He whipped around, cold ice in his eyes. "You *used* me. You probed right into my head. Into my memories, my past, my dreams, my heart. You got me to say things I have never said to another human being. Ever." He fisted his hand and knocked it against his chest. "I opened up, here. I let you in, *Emily.*" His faced darkened. "How do you think that makes me feel, *doctor?* What does the shrink have to say about *that?*"

Heat flushed her cheeks. "The very fact you did let me in saved you, Jean."

His eyes burned into her, into every little crevice of her brain and body. "Well, thank you, doctor, for coming to my rescue."

"You showed me that you are not what the rest of the world believes you to be, Jean. You are nowhere near evil." She hesitated. "Nothing like your father."

Emotion slashed over his features, then was gone. "That's your *professional* assessment, Dr. Carlin?" Cold anger clipped his words.

"It's personal, Jean. Every damn thing about this mission has been personal. Too personal. That's my problem. That's—" she glanced away "—a serious problem," she said, barely audibly.

"Well, you better sort yourself out before you take another job and start sleeping with your next target."

She winced inwardly and emotion burned into her eyes. "If it matters at all to you what I think, you're like your mother, Jean. You have her empathy and her elegance without her fragility." She looked up into his eyes. "And you're like your sister. She was a soldier. She burned with the same fire and determination as you. She also marched to her own drum. She was brave. Bold."

Emotion tore through into his features again, lingering in the glint in his eyes.

Her throat tightened at the rawness she saw in his face. "You're a damn fine person, Jean. Larger than life, bolder than most men could ever dream to be, and more honorable…and…" She looked down at her hands. "And more than most women could ever hope to have known," she said softly.

He didn't speak.

She lifted her eyes slowly, met his, and the memories of their intimacy surged between them, alive like a separate pulsing entity, crackling with the same electricity and pressure as the mounting storm.

"Is it true," he said quietly, "what you told me about your own father? Or was that just another ploy to get me to open up so you could pick at my brain?"

"It's true. Not his profession. He's not a fire chief—"

He turned sharply away.

"It's not the little details that mattered, Jean! I couldn't tell you those without blowing my cover, but the rest of it was all real. My father is a retired U.S. Army general. His name is Tom Carlin."

His back stiffened.

She had a desperate need to tell him the truth, all of it, give him as many facts as he could check. She wanted his trust. She wanted some small sense of reconnection before those choppers she could hear in the distance landed and took her away.

"And yes, I do blame him for my mother's death. And yes, I still love my dad. I don't *like* him, but some sad part of me has always needed him. Like my mother, I have always craved his approval, his affection. I joined the army to win his respect, on his own turf, but he was a hard man to please. I studied the psychology of alpha males and their codependents to better understand him and my mother. I left the army, got my doctorate and went on to become a specialist in tyrannical pathology. And while I enjoy some global renown in highly academic circles for my expertise, while I'm an independent adult with my own means, some sick part of me still seeks the approval of my father for every damn thing I do in my life …" Her voice grew small, almost indistinct. "Which scares the hell out of me."

She paused. "And you can check it. All of it. It's who I am."

He turned slowly to face her. "And you think this makes you somehow weak?"

She nodded.

"You're not weak."

"I am. And I screwed up. I keep screwing up because of this problem I can't seem to get out of my system."

He studied her intensely. "What do you mean?"

The beat of the choppers in the humid air grew louder, closer. Urgency rustled through her. "It's not just my father, Jean. I am habitually attracted to domineering men. Just as my mom was attracted to my dad. And then just when my relationships start getting serious, I think I subconsciously find ways to sabotage them. And I flee, I run, as if for my life, and I try to pretend it's the guy's fault, that he's trying to control my life, that's he's somehow *wrong*." She swallowed, the sound of the helicopters drawing closer, tension winding tighter. "What's wrong is *me,* Jean. I'm stuck in a pathological loop. I seriously screwed up back home, and I should have faced things. Instead I came here, and I fell for you. There. You have it. All of it. And I let it get in the way of my job."

She sucked in a shaky breath. "I've never told a soul. Not straight up like this. I…I never even admitted it to myself. And…" Her voice faltered. "And I'm sorry. I'm supposed to be a therapist," she muttered.

He studied her with cool, probing eyes. "Everything else is true?"

"What we had was real. That was true."

And now it was gone.

He nodded curtly and turned away. As if his need had been satisfied and she'd been dismissed for good.

Her heart bottomed out.

"You…you do understand, don't you?" she said.

He said nothing.

She could see the helicopter lights now, coming

over the black shape of the jungle canopy. The sound of the blades filled the air. Desperation surged in her. "If you'd just have let me finish typing you'd have seen that I believe you."

"Prove it," he said suddenly.

"What?"

He spun round to face her.

"If it's all true, Emily, prove it to me. Stay."

Confusion washed through her. "I don't underst—"

"Stay here in Ubasi. Help me through this. Help me win this war. Help me make it safe enough to bring back the royal family. Help *us* bring democracy to Ubasi." He stepped close, his voice growing low, seductive, aggressive with longing. "If you truly mean what you've just said, use the contacts you have and help me achieve my sister's dream for my people. For me. Right here at my side. *Show* me, Emily, that what we had really was true."

Her heart swooped up in a wild and dizzying roller-coaster lurch, and then plunged right back down the other side in a terrifying free fall.

He wanted commitment from her.

He was forcing her to choose between his life and hers. It was either his cause in Ubasi or her life in Manhattan.

Why did it always have to be like that?

There was no middle ground for this man, and she knew there would never be. He was too strong. Too dominant. Too determined.

And she was suddenly inexplicably terrified.

She jerked back in shock as an explosion rocked the ground just beyond the palace walls. The choppers closed in, filling the air with sound and hot vibration.

A barrage of gunfire peppered the sky.

"They're getting closer," she whispered. "Jacques's men, fighting with Souleyman."

"They've come to take you," he said, eyes not budging from hers.

Another shell hit, the impact reverberating through the stone walls. Panic tightened her throat. The heat and pressure was overwhelming. Another explosion pulsed through the dense air, and she heard the choppers coming in to land in the palace grounds.

Yelling broke out down in the courtyard, Laroque's men pulling back gates, letting FDS soldiers in as they fought back insurgents. She could hear boots clapping up the stairs, pounding down the corridor, growing louder. Wind began to whip fat drops in through the open window as the storm closed in.

His eyes never wavered. "Make your choice, Emily."

The doors swung open. "Carlin! You okay?"

She couldn't speak. Couldn't move.

"We've got orders to get you out ASAP, back to São Diogo. Chopper's waiting!"

One hovered right outside the window, searchlights illuminating the castle walls and grounds, the *thuck thuck thuck* sound pounding through the humid air, slamming through her head.

His eyes lanced hers, not even bothering to look

at the two FDS soldiers who'd burst into his room. Slowly he extended his hand to her. An offer. A bridge. A connection. Steady. Strong. A different life.

She stared at it, heart racing, perspiration prickling over her forehead, trickling down between her breasts.

"*Carlin!* You coming? Pilot needs to move before the storm closes in."

"Jean…I…I need to go back to São Diogo for debriefing. I…I can return. We can see if—"

"It's now or never, Emily." His hand remained steady, palm up. A test.

Indecision immobilized her. Shots rang out again. The sound of the helicopter outside grew deafening. She couldn't think. Her head began to buzz. Suddenly she was completely out of her depth and shaken by everything. Shaken to her foundations as if she was a little girl again.

"Carlin, we need to move ASAP! The storm is closing in!"

"Jean…I *must*…"

He dropped his hand, spun abruptly away from her. He stared out the window, rigid as a stone sculpture, an image of both power and desperate solitude.

It was how he'd lived all his life. Unbearable compassion washed over her, sorrow for what she had done to him. She was so conflicted she felt ill. She loved him. Yes she truly loved this larger-than-life man, in an absurd larger-than-life way. Yet she was still afraid of him. Of *herself.* Of what she could allow him to become in her life, of losing her autonomy, of turning into her mother. She just couldn't make a huge all-or-nothing decision like this. Not in a few seconds.

"Jean?" she whispered, tears filling her eyes.

"Go!"

The single word slammed into her chest like a bullet. She sagged slightly.

Jacques's men took her arm, urging her away gently.

Tears began to stream down Emily's cheeks, and she let Jacques's men take her away.

Forever.

Chapter 15

One week later. CIA director's home.
Washington, D.C.

CIA director Blake Weston stared out his living room window into the dark night sky. Things had gone sideways in Ubasi, and the White House wanted answers ASAP.

It could cost him his job.

Blake had needed Laroque dead, and Souleyman in power. If Laroque had been assassinated in a coup, Washington might have believed that Laroque had discovered the CIA agents' identities on his own, and killed them all as a warning to the West to stay out of his country.

Instead, Souleyman had died in the fighting, and Blake was now faced with Laroque looking like the good guy, along with allegations that a covert faction of the ruling Chinese communist party had killed the agents.

But there was no proof such a Chinese faction even existed. All they had was Laroque's word and the word of his rebels. Blake needed to keep it that way, for reasons of his own.

However, once the so-called mercenaries Laroque's rebels had abducted from Nigeria were interrogated by U.S. forces, proof might indeed surface that they had been contracted by the Chinese to kill the CIA agents. It would also then become apparent that someone *inside* the CIA must have leaked the identities of those agents to the Chinese faction.

That meant serious trouble for Blake. Washington would see it for what it was—a mole somewhere deep within his agency.

Blake had to be seen to be moving swiftly to exorcise this informant. But if he failed to deliver the mole, he was damn well going to need another plan if he was to keep his post as CIA chief.

Blake turned as he heard his wife Shan enter the living room.

"You okay, honey?" she asked, handing him his drink, her long dark hair shimmering in the firelight.

Blake's chest tightened.

Shan had a way of changing his world when she

walked into a room. There was little he wouldn't do for his wife, and little he wouldn't share with her.

"I'm okay." He smiled wryly. "Just hassled about the Sino-African issue."

She touched his face, her exotic almond eyes luminous. "You'll be fine," she said. "You always are. You just have to make sure those captives *don't* talk."

Eleven months later. Late October.
Manhattan

A dense shroud of fog closed in around Manhattan's skyscrapers, socking the city in, making the world even more gray in the early twilight.

Rain flicked against the misted windows of the small café where Emily waited in line for her coffee as she halfheartedly watched the news on the television set above the counter. It was Friday evening, and she was going home to work. Again.

She took her latte from the barista, eyes suddenly glued to the news as coverage segued to a reporter in Ubasi covering the country's first-ever democratic elections.

Her pulse quickened. Coffee in hand, Emily moved closer to the set, riveted by the images of the hot country being transported right into her cold, gray, autumn world.

"The final tallies are now in," said the reporter, holding her ear and speaking into the microphone over the noise of jubilant crowds. Behind her, people were waving banners, chanting, ululating—the same haunting sounds that had assaulted Emily in the dusty streets of Basaroutou on that first day of her mission. The day she'd first laid eyes on Jean-Charles Laroque.

"Mangosutu Mephetwe has been elected the first president of Ubasi in a landslide victory in this small, oil-rich nation's first democratic elections," said the reporter. "The election was marked by long lines that sometimes stretched for miles as people waited patiently at polling booths around the country. Many had traveled for days from interior jungle villages to reach the polling stations, but it was a day unmarked by the violence that has plagued this country for the last three decades, one that will go down in history for the people of this war-torn country."

Goose bumps chased over Emily's skin, and moisture filled her eyes. He'd done it. He'd really done it. She smiled at the television as tears threatened to spill down her cheeks. *"Good for you, Jean,"* she whispered softly to herself. "Good for Ubasi."

She dug into her coat pocket for a tissue, and blew her nose. Then she pulled her coat closed, and stepped out into the cold evening, feeling more alone than she could ever remember. As she walked down the pavement, rain dampening her hair, she reminded herself she'd vowed not to look back, not to regret.

But it was hard not to.

More than anything, it was the irony that got to her. She'd made a habit of sabotaging her relationships with the alpha males she was habitually attracted to—because of her fear that she'd end up like her mom. And then Anthony had brought it all to a head by making a mockery of her pathology, hurting and humiliating Emily in the deepest way. So she'd fled. She'd *run* from her issues again. This time running right out of the country, slap-bang into the biggest Alpha Dog of them all.

And he'd trapped her for good.

Jean-Charles Laroque had made it impossible to run again. And in falling for Le Diable, Emily had been forced to finally confront her fear. For the first time in her life, she'd been able to fully articulate what she'd been doing to herself, and why.

As a therapist Emily knew what kind of catharsis that brought for her patients. Finally recognizing what it was that troubled them was often enough to make the problem go away, or at least give the clients tools to deal appropriately with their issues.

It had been no different for her. The catharsis she'd found in confronting Jean—a walking, breathing image of her fears—and articulating to him what she was truly afraid of, had finally freed her.

But she'd lost him in the process.

That's what ate at her.

Emily knew now that Jean was no tyrant. Yes, he was a potently powerful alpha. But he was a warrior, not an abuser. Jean had not been able to hurt her under the most extreme circumstances of betrayal and war—even though his men had *expected* it of him—and *that* told Emily he would never hurt her like her father had hurt her mother.

She stopped at a traffic light, still clutching her untouched coffee, the world around her a blur of cars and cabs and throngs of pedestrians, horns blaring and tires crackling on rain-smeared streets.

Emily could see now that much of Jean's power came from the mind, not violence. He was a master chess player, a shrewd manipulator. And when he did fight, the battle was always fair, and he sought to win on equal terms. The analyst in Emily could see all this in retrospect—Jean-Charles Laroque lived for challenge, not exploitation of the weak. He supported the disenfranchised in the same way he upheld his sister's dream and fought for the Ubasi people and their king.

She'd seen it in the way Jean had shown his love for those villagers, and for his land.

Her eyes misted again as she neared her apartment, the wind tugging at her hair and nipping at her cheeks. She'd lost a rare man.

She'd lost him because he'd asked her to commit so suddenly, under such extreme pressure, right in the middle of a war zone. It had been impossible for her to do it at that moment—it would have been wrong.

Yet he was such an all-or-nothing, larger-than-life guy—you were either with him or not. He'd been under stress, too. She'd hurt him badly, and she couldn't hold his impetuousness against him.

She nodded at her doorman as she entered her

building and made her way to the elevators, but he stopped her.

"Emily, someone was here for you."

She turned round, puzzled. She'd been so involved in her work she'd virtually become a recluse these past months. She'd thought she'd be happy this way, but in reality, her work was all she had now. "Who?" she asked, frowning.

"He wouldn't leave his name. Said he'd come back. He's already been by three times. Keeps driving past in a limo."

Emily's heart kicked. No. *It couldn't be.* Why should she even think it?

Her mouth went dry. She handed her coffee cup to the doorman. "Here, can you hold this?" Without thinking, she stepped back out into the rain, eyes searching the street for a limousine.

But there was nothing.

She was being ridiculous. Why would he even come to Manhattan? There was no way he'd be in New York, especially today, when the first president was being elected in his country.

Her heart felt flat, her hair damp. She drew her coat closer against the biting cold and turned to reenter her building. That's when she caught sight of a long black limousine coming around the corner.

Emily froze.

The rain-covered limo pulled up on the opposite curb, and her chest tensed as the door slowly opened.

He climbed out, stood to his full height and

stared at her from across the street. His hair was pulled back in elegant dreadlocks, his dark features exotic among the sea of urbane faces that suddenly looked soft and bland juxtaposed alongside his towering strength.

Jean-Charles Laroque literally telegraphed power and an easy physical confidence. It was no different here in New York than seeing him sitting on the back of that Jeep in Basaroutou. And once again, his eyes were trained directly on her, and on her alone.

He smiled, a slash of piratical white against mocha skin, and he raised his hand in a bold salute.

Wild emotion tore through her body with such force it brought tears to Emily's eyes and rooted her to the spot.

He stepped off the curb and came toward her, his coat billowing out behind him, rain glistening on his dark hair, closing the distance between them without breaking eye contact.

And she braced herself, as if for a bullet headed her way.

"Emily—" He reached for her hands as he neared, his voice the low, resonant African base tinged with French that melted her from the inside out.

"Jean…what…what are you doing here?" Her words came out hoarse. "I…I saw the news. The election. You…you did it, Jean!"

He nodded, satisfaction gleaming in his pale green eyes, a sense of power rolling over him in waves. "*We* did it, Emily," he said, taking her hands in his and drawing her close.

"Why aren't you there? Why didn't *you* run for election like they were all pressing you to?"

"I've done my bit, and it was never my goal to govern." A twinkle of unspeakable mischief sparked in his eyes. "I'm not a tyrant, you see, Dr. Carlin."

She smiled. "Point taken. But I thought you'd want to be there today, with King Douala and the new president. You have a lot to celebrate."

His eyes turned serious. "I came for something that is more important to me now. I came for you."

She swallowed, almost afraid to say anything that might make this moment evaporate in front of her eyes.

"Do you think we might go inside, get out of the rain, perhaps?"

"I…oh, yes, I, of course." She felt nervous, excited, energized, and the cocktail of explosive emotion rocketing through her was affecting her ability to speak. "Would…you like to come up to my apartment?"

His gaze was clear and direct. "I'd like that. Very much."

She hesitated. "What about the car—"

He hooked his arm over her shoulder. "Come. My driver will take care of it. He's got Shaka in there. Shaka needs a walk anyway." Jean raised his hand, made a sign to the driver, and the limo pulled out into the traffic.

"You brought *Shaka?*"

"I'm here to stay awhile."

"In *New York?*"

He tipped his head. "Yes, in New York."

Emily poured Jean a glass of single-malt scotch, and his eyes tracked her every movement in a way that made her limbs feel disjointed.

Their fingers connected as she handed him the tumbler, and heat jolted through her. Emily almost jerked back with surprise at the intensity of the sensation. Just one touch and this man could do things to her no other could. She stepped back slowly, heart racing, and sat opposite him, watching his eyes.

There was something different about him. She could see it in his eyes. There was a luminosity she hadn't noticed before. "You look relaxed, Jean. At peace." And even more beautiful.

"I am at peace," he said, his smile reaching right into his eyes in a way that made them twinkle—and her heart spasm. "And you, Emily? How are *you?*"

She glanced down at the whiskey in her glass. "I'm fine. Doing well. Working hard." What else was there to say—*missing you like hell?*

He leaned forward suddenly, his energy intense. "Do you want to know why I'm at peace?"

"Because you have achieved a dream few men could?"

"Because of *you.*"

She frowned.

"You helped show me something I needed to see more than anything else in this world."

"I…I don't understand."

"The therapist in you should." He paused. "We all know what my father did, Emily. He was a brutal murderer and sexual sadist. While he used the arena of war to disguise his crimes—to hide—he was no different from a serial killer in an urban environment."

"You're right," Emily said quietly, trying to read his eyes.

"Well, I am the offspring of that man, and as with the child of any serial killer, there's always the fear that the genetic echo of a murderer lurks deep within him, too." He swirled his whiskey, concentrating on the gold liquid as ice chinked softly against the crystal. "You worry that, given a certain set of circumstances, the killer in you will be set free, too." He looked up. "In essence, you live in fear of *yourself.* Every time you get heated, passionate, angry, you are terrified it might be happening. You don't know what the emotions are supposed to feel like. You don't know if it's normal." He took a deep sip of his drink.

"Well, you took me to the edge of my fear, Emily. You forced me to look right over into that abyss, and you know what?" He grinned, his teeth impossibly white against his skin. "The devil did not look back at me. You showed me that, when pushed to the most extreme circumstances, when faced with a most hurtful and intimate betrayal that almost cost my nation, I was still unable to hurt you. Or anyone. I can't hurt people like he did, and I never will. I know that now. And *that,* Emily, has brought me peace. For that I am extremely grateful."

"I never set out to hurt you, Jean."

"I know that."

She studied him for a long time, and he met her scrutiny. Silence consumed the room, the air growing thick, charged.

"And I know you don't have one ounce of Peter Laroque's evil in you, Jean," she said finally, setting her drink carefully on the coffee table between them. "There was a point I was afraid you did—that you might kill me when you discovered who I really was. But at the end, when you were interrogating me, I saw the way your hand went for your knife. I saw the way you hesitated—how you couldn't draw it from the sheath despite the rage in your eyes. I knew then that you could never hurt me. Even after what I had done to you."

His features turned grave. "I am sorry if I frightened you."

She nodded. "Psychological power, that's your strength, Jean."

"And does *that* worry you, Emily?"

"I… Why should it?"

"You told me about your fears. Your relationships, how you sabotaged them."

Adrenaline skittered through her stomach. "We… we don't have a relationship, Jean. There's no reason it should worry me."

"What if I told you I would like to start one?"

Emotion surged sharply though her chest, and her world shifted slightly. "Jean, I've worked through a lot of things over this past year. I've confronted my issues because of what we went through in Ubasi. I faced them, talked them out, and I've come out the other side a stronger person. But I can't get involved with you."

His features shifted, and so did his energy. "Why not?"

"It won't work, you and me. Our lives are literally worlds apart. My work is here, yours is—"

His eyes narrowed sharply. "What's the real reason, Emily?" His voice was gruff.

Her pulse quickened, and she looked at her hands. "It's not because of my old fears. I can't do it because…because I think I'm in love with you, and you will end up breaking my heart when you go back to your life."

"Emily." He surged to his feet, came round the coffee table and sat on the sofa beside her, grasping her shoulders. "Look at me, Emily."

She lifted her eyes slowly and met his.

"You *know* me. Better than anyone else in this world. You understand who I am—that I am a man of dreams. Big, bold, brash ones. Do you want to know what my next dream is?"

Uncertainty washed through her.

"I wasn't going to tell you the big picture, because I haven't figured out all the pieces yet, and I didn't want to scare you away." His eyes tunneled into hers. "I didn't want you to feel cornered, because you've been so honest in telling me your fears. But I *am* a big-picture guy, and my dream goes well beyond a fling, Emily."

"Jean, I—"

He raised his hand. "No, listen to me. *Then* you can turn me down. If you want, I will walk out that door and never come back, because the last thing in the world I want to do is to make you feel trapped, Emily." He paused. "Or to ask you to sacrifice your autonomy in any way whatsoever. Will you hear me out?"

She nodded, her mouth dry.

"A ranch—" he said, standing up to his full height, stretching out his hand, painting the vision in his mind. "Acres and acres of Ubasi land as far as your eye can see. And up there, on the hill—" he pointed to an imaginary space "—a house overlooking a sugar-white beach, surf rolling like thunder along the shore, throwing white spindrift into the wind." His eyes locked on hers, his energy visceral, magnetic. "And that house, Emily, is where I will bring my wife, where we will raise *our* children, in a free nation—a place I helped build with my own blood and sweat. A place to belong. A home." He lowered himself onto the sofa beside her. "A place, Emily, that you helped me build." He stilled, eyes lancing hers. "And I want you to be my wife."

Her mouth opened, and emotion flooded to her eyes.

"You see? I didn't want to tell you this. I wanted to go one day at a time. But I also want you to know that I don't want to go back to Ubasi without you."

Emily began to tremble inside. "Jean, I…I don't know what to say. I can't go. My work is here. Everything of mine is here."

Insecurity ripped through his eyes, and his mouth flattened. It was the first time Emily had glimpsed this unfamiliar emotion in him.

"I took an apartment in Manhattan," he said tonelessly. "I have business here—my offshore investments, my oil interests. I have United Nations meetings to attend—I accepted a temporary post as Ubasi ambassador to the U.N. until they find someone else. Until I know if you want to be with me."

"You did this all for me, Jean?"

He shrugged, a vulnerability in his eyes. "I'm afraid that scares you, Emily. I go hard for my dreams. But I want you to understand—" he said, cupping her face so tenderly "—that even though I fought *hard* for my country, it now stands free. That's how I see us—a hard-won union. Strong together, yet always free. Always together."

She brushed away the tear that had spilled onto her cheek. "You really do nothing in half measures, do you?"

His eyes suddenly turned fierce. "I do. I *can*. Watch me. One day at a time. Baby steps. How about it, Emily? Anytime you want to step away, anytime you feel closed in, you are free to walk, and I will let you. I promise you that. I would never, ever ask you to be where you don't want. But this must be *your* choice."

She bit her lip, her heart bursting with such a powerfully raw love she could barely restrain it. After this past year, after working through her problems, after missing him so damn badly, all she wanted to do was say yes, and be with him.

But she was afraid to make that mistake.

"Jean, what about my work? I can't just give it all up." But even as Emily mouthed the words, she was thinking about the offer Jacques Sauvage had made her last month. He needed a therapist on call full-time for his growing private army on São Diogo. He wanted someone who understood the mindset of a soldier—someone who could handle complex psychological debriefings when needed. This, Jacques had said, would be in addition to her regular FDS profiling contracts. Emily had been sorely tempted, but unsure about permanently relocating to that part of the world.

But Ubasi was close to São Diogo, an hour or two max by military chopper. Maybe it *was* a viable alternative. Maybe she should try this all on for size, like Jean said, one baby step at a time. An uncontainable excitement began to build in her.

She looked at him, unable to temper the animation in her eyes. This was a man who would fight to the death to defend her, yet never hurt her. He would protect her right to freedom, just as she'd seen him do for his country.

Jean was more man than a woman could ever hope for.

Emily had vowed she would do something fresh

in her life—something new and exciting—if she ever made it out of Ubasi alive. Perhaps this was it. She just hadn't thought she might return to Africa to fulfill that promise she'd made to herself. She told herself this was not about looking back. This was about going forward. Leaving all her old paranoia behind her while taking a step in a bold new direction.

With the man who had shown her how to do that.

Jean was watching her face intently. The hope etched into his features touched her heart.

She nodded, tears suddenly streaming down her cheeks, even as she smiled.

He closed his eyes, a barely perceptible shudder running through his muscular frame. When he opened them, his relief was clear, raw. Emily began to laugh and sob at the same time, and he grabbed her, kissing her deeply and hard and completely.

He broke away and tenderly wiped the tears from her cheeks. "We should celebrate. Where do you like to go in Manhattan on a Friday night?"

Emily realized with mild alarm that she hadn't been out in months. While her work and the writing of her new book were going great, she'd had such a pathetic excuse for a social life, she was at a complete loss as to where she'd like to go. "How about," she said, smiling, "I cook you dinner?"

"Here?"

"Right here, in my apartment."

His eyes twinkled. "You cook?"

"Very well, actually."

He looked into her eyes, a warm appreciation and wonder blooming in his own. "I know you so intimately," he said softly, his voice husky. "Yet there are so many more things to discover." He traced the line of her face with his fingers as he spoke, and the seduction in his tone snaked warm and slow through her. She swallowed, her body tingling deep inside.

"One day at a time, Jean," she whispered, leaning forward and brushing her mouth over his.

A soft moan escaped his chest as her lips feathered his. Jean wrapped his arms around her and threw back his head, closing his eyes tight as emotion swam sharp and sweet behind his lids. For the first time since he could remember, he felt the impulse to cry.

He had finally gotten everything he had searched for. A country where he belonged; a place he could call home.

And beyond all that, in his arms he held a woman he not only loved with every molecule in his body, but a woman he respected as his equal. One of the strongest women he had ever met.

A woman who knew him better than anyone in this world—one he hoped to one day start a family with. The thought filled his belly with hot pleasure. He tilted her chin up and kissed her. "One day at a time," he murmured, and that's how he was going to hold on to her.

Forever.

Epilogue

Eighteen months later.
Ubasi Palace grounds

Laroque slipped his arm around Emily's waist, drawing her to his side as they stood by the dark waters of the rockpool in the Ubasi Palace gardens, greeting guests.

King Douala was hosting a lavish royal engagement celebration for Laroque and Emily. The night was sultry and heady with tropical fragrance. Torches lit the palace gardens. Drums beat, and tribal dancers entertained guests under a brilliant starry sky.

Things had stabilized in Ubasi. The economy was on the upswing and the first democratic elections had been an unquestionable success. President Mangosutu Mephetwe—the headman and friend who'd warned Laroque about the high priestess's prophecy—had established a solid cabinet, and encouraged a healthy opposition.

In the meantime, Laroque and King Douala had managed to broker groundbreaking treaties with neighboring governments and multinational oil corporations, and dates had been set for the first-ever official Niger Delta talks with the new Africa Oil Cartel.

Dignitaries from those neighboring countries were in attendance tonight, as was President Mephetwe. The high priestess herself was at the party, along with key rebel leaders and FDS boss Jacques Sauvage and his wife, Olivia. Also on hand for the celebration was a crew from *Vanity Fair,* who were doing a glossy spread on the "Manhattan psychologist and her mercenary" to coincide with the release of Emily's new book.

Over the past eighteen months Laroque had worked closely with Emily on her book, which had evolved to focus on the key psychological indicators that determined who might become a diabolical despot versus a truly powerful leader—be it in politics, war, business or relationships. She'd used Le Diable and the Ubasi story as the primary case study, contrasting Laroque's unorthodox rule to the reigns of African despots who'd achieved less happy outcomes.

Laroque had agreed to pose, with Shaka, for the cover, his mesmerizing green eyes and strikingly

powerful dark features enticing—almost *daring*—
readers to pick up the timely hardcover, which hit a
readership hungry for a radical success story in the
current environment of economic downturn and
global bad news.

In many ways, the book had become Laroque's
public absolution. Emily herself was thrilled the
world could now see her fiancé for the sensitive and
peace-loving man he really was. Above all, Emily
hoped the phenomenal publicity they were getting
would help generate even more funding for the foundation she and Jean had started to support and reha-
bilitate child soldiers.

Her new clinic on their Ubasi ranch would serve
as a refuge for many of those young soldiers—mere
boys who had been driven into war in much the same
way Laroque had been at age thirteen. It was serious
work. Emily was also contracting to the FDS in a
therapeutic capacity for Jacques's mercenaries, who
suffered from varying degrees of PTSD, or who
needed professional debriefing in other ways. She
was ideally suited to this role, given her own military
background and her relationship to Jean.

But there was more than their love and Ubasi's
future to celebrate tonight. Emily was pregnant, and
Laroque could not have been more thrilled at the
prospect of having his child born right here in his
country—a symbol of the new era of hope, a bridge
over the chasm of African and Western ideology.

Both he and Emily had agreed that if the baby was a girl, her name would be Tamasha.

Jacques caught Emily's and Laroque's attention as they made their way through the garden, and he drew them aside for a moment. "Congratulations again on the engagement." He smiled.

"Thanks in part to you," said Laroque, grinning. "You sent her my way."

Jacques slapped Laroque on the back. "You did good by her. And it's always nice to make a new ally, *mon ami*."

"Still no news on that alleged covert arm of the Beijing government?" Laroque asked as they walked up the lawn together.

Jacques stopped, glanced over his shoulder and lowered his voice. "Everything points to a force operating behind the scenes for the Chinese, and not just in Africa," he said. "But we have no *proof*. Not since the U.S. convoy transporting those mercs you captured came under attack. All evidence died with them."

"Do you have any idea who attacked them?" asked Emily.

"Not yet. It looked like renegades, but we assume it was Chinese-backed, and that they were tipped off about the convoy." He lowered his voice further. "Between us, we think there's a mole deep in the CIA itself. Someone is *still* feeding highly sensitive information directly to Beijing."

"What's Blake Weston doing about it?"

"He's done what he can," said Jacques. "There's been an inquiry. He fired a few people to appease Washington brass, and he kept his job. But otherwise, the leads have gone stone-cold. Until *now*." He paused, making doubly sure no one was eavesdropping. "Some very interesting information has just come out of Vancouver on Canada's west coast. Weston has asked us to look into it. He wants to appear completely hands-off on this, because he can't trust his own right now."

"So he's outsourced this to the FDS?" said Emily.

"Correct."

"What kind of information?" asked Laroque.

"Jessica Chan, a BBC foreign correspondent who used to be stationed in Shanghai, must know something because she appears to have been targeted by this organization. She's gone to ground, and we need to find her before they do."

"So this woman could provide proof that this organization exists?"

Jacques nodded. "*Oui*. And she could potentially lead us right to the mole. My key Pacific Rim operative, Luke Stone, has been dispatched to handle the case." He paused. "That proof—when and *if* Stone gets it—has the potential to change the world's political climate. If the Communist party really is working behind the scenes for global domination while pretending to play nice at international negotiation tables, we're looking at another Cold War scenario here."

Jacques slapped Laroque's shoulder. "But there is a time for everything, and tonight we must celebrate our achievements—and your happiness. Let's go back to the party. I hear King Douala has fireworks planned."

Jean winked at Emily, and she returned his smile as they linked hands and walked up the palace lawn to greet their guests in a land they had made their home.

* * * * *

Don't miss the next chapter in
Loreth Anne White's exciting
SHADOW SOLDIERS *miniseries*
THE HEART OF A RENEGADE
On sale March 2008
wherever Silhouette Books are sold.

SPECIAL EDITION®

LIFE, LOVE AND FAMILY

*These contemporary romances will strike
a chord with you as heroines juggle life
and relationships on their way to true love.*

New York Times *bestselling author*
Linda Lael Miller
*brings you a BRAND-NEW contemporary story
featuring her fan-favorite McKettrick family.*

Meg McKettrick is surprised to be reunited with
her high school flame, Brad O'Ballivan. After
enjoying a career as a country-and-western
singer, Brad aches for a home and family…and
seeing Meg again makes him realize he still
loves her. But their pride manages to interfere
with love…until an unexpected matchmaker
gets involved.

Turn the page for a sneak preview of
THE McKETTRICK WAY
by Linda Lael Miller
On sale November 20
wherever books are sold.

Brad shoved the truck into gear and drove to the bottom of the hill, where the road forked. Turn left, and he'd be home in five minutes. Turn right, and he was headed for Indian Rock.

He had no damn business going to Indian Rock.

He had nothing to say to Meg McKettrick, and if he never set eyes on the woman again, it would be two weeks too soon.

He turned right.

He couldn't have said why.

He just drove straight to the Dixie Dog Drive-In.

Back in the day, he and Meg used to meet at the Dixie Dog, by tacit agreement, when either of them had been away. It had been some kind of universe thing, purely intuitive.

Passing familiar landmarks, Brad told himself he ought to turn around. The old days were gone. Things had ended badly between him and Meg anyhow, and she wasn't going to be at the Dixie Dog.

He kept driving.

He rounded a bend, and there was the Dixie Dog. Its big neon sign, a giant hot dog, was all lit up and going through its corny sequence—first it was covered in red squiggles of light, meant to suggest ketchup, and then yellow, for mustard.

Brad pulled into one of the slots next to a speaker, rolled down the truck window and ordered.

A girl roller-skated out with the order about five minutes later.

When she wheeled up to the driver's window, smiling, her eyes went wide with recognition, and she dropped the tray with a clatter.

Silently Brad swore. Damn if he hadn't forgotten he was a famous country singer.

The girl, a skinny thing wearing too much eye makeup, immediately started to cry. "I'm sorry!" she sobbed, squatting to gather up the mess.

"It's okay," Brad answered quietly, leaning to look down at her, catching a glimpse of her plastic name tag. "It's okay, Mandy. No harm done."

"I'll get you another dog and a shake right away, Mr. O'Ballivan!"

"Mandy?"

She stared up at him pitifully, sniffling. Thanks to the copious tears, most of the goop on her eyes had slid south. "Yes?"

"When you go back inside, could you not mention seeing me?"

"But you're Brad O'Ballivan!"

"Yeah," he answered, suppressing a sigh. "I know."

She rolled a little closer. "You wouldn't happen to have a picture you could autograph for me, would you?"

"Not with me," Brad answered.

"You could sign this napkin, though," Mandy said. "It's only got a little chocolate on the corner."

Brad took the paper napkin and her order pen, and scrawled his name. Handed both items back through the window.

She turned and whizzed back toward the side entrance to the Dixie Dog.

Brad waited, marveling that he hadn't considered incidents like this one before he'd decided to come back home. In retrospect, it seemed shortsighted, to say the least, but the truth was, he'd expected to be— Brad O'Ballivan.

Presently Mandy skated back out again, and this time she managed to hold on to the tray.

"I didn't tell a soul!" she whispered. "But Heather and Darlene *both* asked me why my mascara was all smeared." Efficiently she hooked the tray onto the bottom edge of the window.

Brad extended payment, but Mandy shook her head.

"The boss said it's on the house, since I dumped your first order on the ground."

He smiled. "Okay, then. Thanks."

Mandy retreated, and Brad was just reaching for the food when a bright red Blazer whipped into the space beside his. The driver's door sprang open, crashing into the metal speaker, and somebody got out in a hurry.

Something quickened inside Brad.

And in the next moment Meg McKettrick was standing practically on his running board, her blue eyes blazing.

Brad grinned. "I guess you're not over me after all," he said.

REQUEST YOUR FREE BOOKS!

2 FREE NOVELS PLUS 2 FREE GIFTS!

Silhouette® Romantic

SUSPENSE

Sparked by Danger, Fueled by Passion!

YES! Please send me 2 FREE Silhouette® Romantic Suspense novels and my 2 FREE gifts. After receiving them, if I don't wish to receive any more books, I can return the shipping statement marked "cancel." If I don't cancel, I will receive 4 brand-new novels every month and be billed just $4.24 per book in the U.S., or $4.99 per book in Canada, plus 25¢ shipping and handling per book plus applicable taxes, if any*. That's a savings of at least 15% off the cover price! I understand that accepting the 2 free books and gifts places me under no obligation to buy anything. I can always return a shipment and cancel at any time. Even if I never buy another book from Silhouette, the two free books and gifts are mine to keep forever.

240 SDN EEX6   340 SDN EEYJ

Name   (PLEASE PRINT)

Address   Apt. #

City   State/Prov.   Zip/Postal Code

Signature (if under 18, a parent or guardian must sign)

Mail to the **Silhouette Reader Service™:**

IN U.S.A.: P.O. Box 1867, Buffalo, NY 14240-1867
IN CANADA: P.O. Box 609, Fort Erie, Ontario L2A 5X3

Not valid to current Silhouette Intimate Moments subscribers.

Want to try two free books from another line?
Call 1-800-873-8635 or visit www.morefreebooks.com.

* Terms and prices subject to change without notice. NY residents add applicable sales tax. Canadian residents will be charged applicable provincial taxes and GST. This offer is limited to one order per household. All orders subject to approval. Credit or debit balances in a customer's account(s) may be offset by any other outstanding balance owed by or to the customer. Please allow 4 to 6 weeks for delivery.

Your Privacy: Silhouette is committed to protecting your privacy. Our Privacy Policy is available online at www.eHarlequin.com or upon request from the Reader Service. From time to time we make our lists of customers available to reputable firms who may have a product or service of interest to you. If you would prefer we not share your name and address, please check here. ☐

SRS07

Get ready to meet

THREE WISE WOMEN

with stories by

DONNA BIRDSELL, LISA CHILDS

and

SUSAN CROSBY.

Don't miss these three unforgettable stories about modern-day women and the love and new lives they find on Christmas.

Look for *Three Wise Women*
Available December wherever you buy books.

ATHENA FORCE

Heart-pounding romance and thrilling adventure.

She's their ace in the hole.

Posing as a glamorous high roller, Bethany James, a professional gambler and sometimes government agent, uncovers a mob boss's deadly secrets…and the ugly sins from his past. But when a daredevil with a tantalizing drawl calls her bluff, the stakes—and her heart rate—become much, much higher. Beth can't help but wonder: Have the cards been finally stacked against her?

ATHENA FORCE

Will the women of Athena unravel Arachne's powerful web of blackmail and death…or succumb to their enemies' deadly secrets?

Look for

STACKED DECK
by *Terry Watkins.*

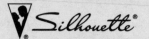

Romantic

SUSPENSE

COMING NEXT MONTH

#1491 HER SWORN PROTECTOR—Marie Ferrarella
The Doctors Pulaski
Cardiologist Kady Pulaski is the only witness to a billionaire shipping magnate's murder. Now the former billionaire's bodyguard, Byron Kennedy, must keep Kady alive long enough to testify against the killer. But can he withstand his attraction to the fiery doctor?

#1492 LAZLO'S LAST STAND—Kathleen Creighton
Mission: Impassioned
When a series of violent attacks afflicts the Lazlo Group, security expert Corbett Lazlo asks Lucia Cordez to play his lover to lure the assassins out of hiding. And as the escalating threat forces them to hole up in intimate quarters, their growing feelings for each other could be an even greater danger.

#1493 DEADLY TEMPTATION—Justine Davis
Redstone, Incorporated
Redstone agent Liana Kiley is stunned to discover that the heroic lawman who saved her life years ago is wanted for corruption...and she's determined to investigate the case. Detective Logan Beck is not happy about dragging Liana back into danger, but with a perfect frame closing in around him, he must put his life—and heart—in her hands.

#1494 THE MEDUSA SEDUCTION—Cindy Dees
The Medusa Project
To catch one of the world's most dangerous terrorists, army captain Brian Riley must abduct and transform civilian Sophie Giovanni into a commando. Sophie is the one woman who can identify Brian's target, but with time running out he must choose between his loyalty to his agency and the woman who's stolen his heart.